The Pot Thief Who Studied Einstein

The Pot Thief
Who Studied
Einstein

A Pot Thief Mystery

J. MICHAEL ORENDUFF

OPEN ROAD

INTEGRATED MEDIA

NEW YORK

Cover design by Kathleen Lynch

ISBN 978-1-4804-5880-2

This edition published in 2014 by Open Road Integrated Media, Inc.
345 Hudson Street
New York, NY 10014
www.openroadmedia.com

This book is dedicated to my father, Jess J. Orenduff (1911-1971),
who taught me that life is to be enjoyed.
I wish I had been a better son.
And to my son, Jay, the best son any man ever had.

The Pot Thief Who Studied Einstein

1

I was trying to remember if I'd ever been blindfolded before.

I didn't think I had been, but the cloth on my eyes felt vaguely familiar, almost nostalgic. I couldn't imagine why. The only images I could connect with blindfolds were kidnappings.

What I *should* have been doing was estimating the distance traveled by the car and memorizing the turns it made. I'd seen that once in an old movie where the person being kidnapped was later able to lead the police to the bad guys' hideout by sitting in the patrol car with his eyes closed, recalling the trip.

"Turn right," he would tell them. Then he would fall silent and intent as if counting to himself. "Turn left," he would direct after the appropriate length of time.

Or maybe not. Maybe that works only in movies. Even if you counted at a set cadence and could remember that it was a count of, say, eighty between the second and third turns, that wouldn't tell you how far you had gone unless you also knew how fast the car was traveling.

But I never got a chance to try it because I started wondering whether I'd been blindfolded before.

You might think it foolish of me to be so easily distracted while being kidnapped. Except I wasn't being kidnapped. I had voluntarily agreed to be blindfolded for this ride.

As things turned out, it would have saved me a lot of hassle if I *had* paid attention to where we were going. I almost certainly wouldn't have been arrested for murder.

I'd been told we were going to the home of a reclusive collector of Anasazi pottery. I'm a dealer in ancient pots.

I'm also a pot thief, but I wasn't planning to steal anything. I'd been engaged to give an estimate of the value of the collection, a pleasant evening's work for which the collector had agreed to pay me twenty-five hundred dollars. I would have done it for free just to see the pots, but there was no reason to tell him that.

Anyone with a collection of true Anasazi pots is sitting on a fortune. If he sold the collection—which I had been told was why he wanted an appraisal—the twenty-five hundred would be petty cash to him. But for me, it would pay the mortgage for a few months and keep me stocked in New Mexico's finest champagne, Gruet *Blanc de Noir*.

It was the height of the tourist season in Albuquerque, but I'd sold only one pot from my shop in Old Town. The tourists were out in full force buying dyed corn necklaces, beaded moccasins, cactus candies and rubber rattlesnakes.

Merchandise in the ninety-nine cents to nine-ninety-nine range was flying off the shelves of other stores around the historic plaza, but no one seemed willing to part with the thousand dollars it would take to buy the least expensive item in my store, a small dish from the Acoma Pueblo with their traditional geometric pattern of black lines on a white background.

The dish was unglazed and therefore unsuitable for most practical applications, but it displayed the simplicity and grace typical of Acoma, and I was surprised no one had bought it.

The most expensive piece in my inventory at that time was a squat Anasazi jug with a variety of minor nicks and dings, not to mention a hand-sized hole in its bottom. For those who wanted that pot, but couldn't swing the fifty-thousand-dollar price, I had fashioned a copy identical in all respects to the original, and it was only a tenth of the asking price.

In some ways, it was even better. It didn't have a hole in it, and no politically correct nitwit was going to hassle you about returning it to its rightful owners.

Supply and demand was what they taught me in the University of New Mexico Business School. The supply of originals is low because the Anasazi disappeared about a thousand years ago.

Except there are a few more "originals" out there than there should be because some of my copies have been sold as the genuine article. I know it sounds unethical. But look at it this way. I'm happier because I get a better price, and the buyer is happier because he has the pride of ownership of something he believes is ancient and rare.

Two happy consenting adults.

I've never lied about my copies. I don't label them as genuine. If someone asks if one of them is real, I tell the truth. But if someone buys one off the shelf no-questions-asked, I take the money and wrap up the pot.

Caveat emptor.

The next thing I knew, the car came to a stop and the engine went silent. The driver opened my door and led me by the arm up a walk and into a house. I did notice how far it was from the curb to the door, and that came in handy later.

Sort of.

"Stand here," he said, and I heard him back away and close the door.

A voice from the other side of the room said, "You can remove the blindfold now."

Then I remembered—*piñatas*.

Of course I'd been blindfolded before. Every fifth day of May, from as early as I could remember until I was maybe fourteen years old, there would be a *piñata* at my birthday party.

The memory was bittersweet. The people involved were mostly gone, my parents both deceased, my childhood friends drifted away and my old nanny suffering from kidney disease.

But my cheerful nature quickly reprised the memory. My parents had led long and happy lives. My childhood friends had gone on to the lives they wanted, and we had all made new friends. And maybe the doctors could successfully treat Consuela Sanchez' condition or even do a transplant if it came to that, and she would live to see the grandchild she so desperately wanted.

I pulled myself out of my reverie and responded to the unseen voice by removing the blindfold.

A large misshapen hand held open a swinging door. Between the door and the wall stood the owner of the hand, a stooped fellow with a strong jaw and eyes hidden deep under bushy brows. Above the brows was a big boney forehead complete with a supraorbital ridge the likes of which one rarely sees outside of an anthropology lab.

When I'd been told he was a reclusive collector of Anasazi pottery, I assumed it was his hobby that made him a recluse. There are people out there who believe no one should possess any ancient pottery, and they're not above breaking into houses to achieve their goal. Most of them are just misguided do-gooders, but a few of them are dangerous zealots.

But looking at this contemporary Quasimodo made me wonder if it wasn't his appearance that made him agoraphobic.

"I was told you like margaritas," he said, "so I put one there on the coffee table."

I glanced down and saw the drink. I know this is unfair and probably indicates a character flaw on my part, but my first thought was what kind of poison might be in the drink.

A bottle of Corona sat next to the margarita, and next to that was an opener and a glass with a wedge of lime on its rim.

"If you prefer a beer, I put one of those out too," he added.

He had an Hispanic accent. Nothing unusual about that in Albuquerque, but his was different. His wasn't hard to under-stand—quite the contrary. He pronounced each word carefully as if it were an effort.

"That's very thoughtful of you," I responded. "Maybe I'll have something later, but I think I should keep a clear head while doing the appraisal."

"Okay, but don't leave without a drink. I don't like things to be wasted."

Then you shouldn't have put them out in advance I was tempted to say. What I said instead was, "Are there other pots elsewhere in the house?"

"No," he replied and let the door swing shut.

I was standing on Saltillo tile in a small entry area raised several inches above a living room carpeted in beige. There was a door to the right—a coat closet I assumed—a wrought iron railing to the left, and a step down straight ahead.

The left wall had a fireplace with a stucco mantel and deep floor-to-ceiling shelves on each side that displayed twenty-five pieces of ancient clayware, mostly Anasazi, but with a few works of different origin. Most people wouldn't know the difference. I did.

There was a window in the wall directly opposite the entrance. Its thick cream-colored shade was all the way down but couldn't block the strong desert sun. Even though no lights were on, the room was a clean well-lighted place.

The coffee table with the drinks on it was in the center of the room in front of the fireplace, and a Danish modern couch was against the right wall. There was no other furniture in the room. Maybe the collector spent all his money on pots.

At the far end of the room just past the shelves was the swinging door the man who greeted me had disappeared behind to do whatever he intended to do as I did my work. I half expected to see a portrait on the wall with real eyes peering out at me. I had also seen that a couple of times in old movies, but there was no artwork of any sort on the walls.

Still, you couldn't say the room was austere. No matter how grandiose the décor might have been, the pottery would have rendered it superfluous.

Ancient Native American pottery is more beautiful than gold and almost as expensive. My love affair with it started when I unearthed three pots while on a dig as a graduate student back in the eighties. The money I got for those pots was enough for a down payment on my Old Town adobe, which has my shop in the front and my residence in the back. I love living there, and I love the freedom of being my own boss, but what I love most is my merchandise.

The pottery of the Anasazi and the other pot makers of the pre-historic Southwest is a national treasure. Prospecting for those pots is challenging, finding one is exhilarating, and when we do so, we should be celebrated and rewarded.

It was once thus. Treasure hunters—as we were called back then—enjoyed a glamorous public image, the sort of personae popularized in the last few years by the Indiana Jones films.

Then someone came up with the ridiculous idea that these national treasures didn't belong to all of us, that they belong solely to the descendants of the people who made them, and that those of us who dig them up are dishonoring their makers.

I understand some of the motivation for these ideas. Some treasure hunters behaved badly. Some even dug secretly on reservations.

But most of us felt more reverence for the objects we found than did those who wanted to stop us. After all, it was our awe of the pots that led us to seek them out in the first place. We believe—at least I do—that they deserve to be seen and enjoyed, not left forever in the ground. I'm certain the women who made them would rather have their pottery on display in my shop than have them slowly dissolving back into the clay from whence they came.

But the worst part about this new attitude is that there is not a shred of scientific evidence to suggest that the ancient potters actually *have* descendants. Indeed, the best anthropological evidence suggests that, for example, the Mogollon of the Gila Wilderness died out completely, and no modern day Indians are descended from them.

But Congress caved in to political pressure and passed the Archaeological Resources Protection Act (ARPA) redefining treasure hunting as theft. And as I often quip, who knows more about thievery than Congress?

Despite Congress' efforts, here I was standing awestruck in front of the best collection of Anasazi pots I had ever seen. I thought, as I always do in the presence of these luminous treasures, about the people who made them, about how much I share with them.

We are all potters, people working the clay beneath our feet into the implements of our hands, the tools of civilization—water jugs, storage vessels, plates, and bowls. When I picture those ancient potters, I can feel the wet clay smooth between their fingers. I can see the glow of the fire dancing across their faces. I can sense their pulse quicken as they remove the pot after the fire is cold and see that it is good.

I hope they somehow know how much their work means to me. If they were to see me making pots today, they would understand every step of my process. A thousand years separate us and we speak different tongues. But we have these things in common—the clay, the process, the pride of artisanship.

I reveled in that feeling for several minutes. Then I took from my briefcase a seamstress' tape, a small sketchbook, and a box of pastel pencils and set about earning my pay.

2

Susannah's big brown eyes stared over the rim of her margarita glass, incredulous.

"You let him blindfold you?"

"It was part of the deal. Carl said the guy is paranoid about his collection. He never lets anyone see it."

"But you said it was in plain view in the living room."

"I guess he never has guests."

Business is slow in the high-end pot trade, and Susannah's chores as a lunchtime waitress at La Placita don't allow much time for socializing, so she and I meet most weekdays at five for margaritas at Dos Hermanas Tortillaria where we can get anything that's on our minds off. The topics run the gamut, but frequently deal with her attempts to find Mr. Right and my brushes with the law. She's a couple of inches taller than me and a couple of decades younger, outdoorsy but still very feminine.

It was a typical dry summer day, and I needed another margarita. Actually, I needed a glass of cold water to quench my thirst because I knew where quenching it with margaritas would get me— Jimmy Buffet's favorite town.

So when the willowy Angie made her way through the crowd and over to our usual table, I asked for a large glass of ice water.

And another margarita. The water was a complement, not a substitute.

Susannah ordered more salsa and chips. The salsa at Dos Hermanas Tortillaria is made by hand on site by one of the *hermanas*. I don't know which one because they're usually in the kitchen in their white frocks with their hands covered in masa and their heads covered with old-fashioned hairnets. The front of the house is run by Angie and the hired help, but the sisters don't let anyone but family do the cooking.

The salsa is simple—tomatoes, jalapeños, white onions, and cilantro, finely chopped and seasoned with just a touch of salt and their secret ingredient, lime zest. I make the same recipe at home, but it's never as good, probably because the sisters have a source for real tomatoes whereas I have to use the hydroponic, picked green and ripened-in-the-truck jobs they sell in grocery stores.

Susannah has a theory that the chips soak up alcohol and keep her from getting drunk.

She grabbed the last chip from the bowl before Angie whisked it away and said, "You know what you should have done, Hubie? You should have counted how long you went before each turn and which direction the turns were. Then you could have retraced the route and found out where he lives."

"You must have seen that in an old movie."

"You saw it, too? Humphrey Bogart, right?"

"I don't remember who was in it. Anyway, I was busy doing something else."

"What?"

"I was trying to remember if I'd ever been blindfolded before," I said sheepishly.

"How long could that take? I don't remember you ever telling me about being kidnapped, so . . . Wait! I'll bet you played pin the tail on the donkey at birthday parties, and that's when you were blindfolded."

"Close. It was at birthday parties, but it wasn't pin the tail on the donkey. It was when I got to swing at the *piñata*."

"Bet you were never the one who busted it open."

"How did you know that?"

"You probably couldn't reach it," she said mischievously.

"I wasn't that short then." I'm 5' 6" now and used to the occasional short joke.

"No one's tall in the first grade, but I'll bet you were the shortest one."

"Was not," I said in my little boy voice. "Pudgy Perez was even shorter than me. Wider too."

"I think I could have guessed that. What happened to him?"

"He never got much taller, but he got a lot wider. He's a mechanic. I take my Bronco to him when it needs repairs."

"He must be a genius to keep that thing running. But why did you never hit the *piñata*?"

"My mother said it would be rude for the guest of honor to be the one who broke the *piñata*, so my father would pull the rope when I swung. Then after everyone had a turn or two, he would let one of the other kids clobber the thing without making it look too obvious. He was pretty deft with a *piñata* rope."

I guess my eyes may have clouded over a bit with nostalgia. I stared off into the middle distance.

After a few seconds, Susannah said, "Something bothering you?"

I shrugged. "When I was older, maybe fifteen, Consuela told me the tradition is to let the birthday person break the *piñata*. I was kind of upset."

"You were angry with your parents for not letting you break the *piñata*?"

"Of course not. I was embarrassed that all my friends probably thought my family were dolts because we didn't know the rules about *piñatas* on birthdays."

"That's your worst childhood experience?"

"Hey, it's hard enough fitting in when you're short and don't play sports, but throw in feeling foolish, and—"

"Get over it."

"Yeah, you're right. Anyway, I still had a lot of fun. I remember once when I was about eleven, the *piñata* had mints in it, and when it broke open they showered down on the grass. Lupita Fuentes and I jumped at the same mint, but she grabbed it first and popped it in her mouth. Then she stuck her tongue out with the mint on it."

"Geez," Susannah moaned, "I think I know where this is going."

"Yep. 'You want to taste it?' she said. That was my first kiss."

"Wow," she said sarcastically, "Your first kiss and a French one at that."

"I wonder what happened to Lupita."

"Probably married Pudgy Perez. Can we get back to your blindfolded ride? I don't see how thinking about blindfolds could prevent you from memorizing the route."

"I'm not very good at multitasking. And anyway, I didn't think there was any reason I'd need to go back, so why memorize the route?"

She gave me that enigmatic smile, like the Mona Lisa but without all the crackly lines. "You could have gone back to steal the pots."

I gave her one of my own smiles, the one designed to make me look like the sage humoring an untutored waif, but which Susannah says only makes me look like Joseph Biden.

"I'm not a thief."

The thief debate is a staple of our cocktail hour at Dos Hermanas, as is Susannah's rocky love life, her studies at the University (currently in art history, but subject to change without notice), old movies, and anything else one of us deems worthy.

"There was that pot you took from the University," she reminded me.

"Which was subsequently returned along with a sizeable scholarship fund for students."

"Yeah, but you didn't know that when you took it."

"I had a hunch," I said lamely.

She laughed and took a chug of her margarita larger than Miss Manners recommends for young ladies. Susannah takes hers without salt on the rim. Other than that, she has no flaws.

"Anyway," I added, "you helped me take the thing."

"True," she agreed, "but it's not stealing when an art historian does it."

"I know. You call it 'de-accessioning.'"

"And there was that pot you stole from Hugo Berdal's truck."

"You may recall that Hugo was dead and therefore had no need for the pot, which, incidentally, he had stolen in the first place."

"Quibbling."

"There was something else we took from that truck," I reminded her, "the inflatable woman."

"Yuk, don't remind me."

I sipped my margarita after rotating the glass a few degrees in order to get just the right amount of salt from the rim. It's a subtle but important skill I've honed over the years. When the last hint of the blue agave had faded away, I took a long draw on my water.

"As it turns out, I do want to go back."

"You *are* going to steal his pots!"

"Of course not. But I would like to get my twenty-five hundred dollars back."

"I thought he paid you before you left."

"He did. After I finished, I went over to the swinging door and knocked on it. Without opening the door, he asked me if I was through. I said I was. He asked me if I'd had my margarita or my beer. I told him I hadn't, and he said, 'At least take a drink of one of them while I get the money.' I heard his footsteps recede, and to tell you the truth, I was beginning to think he wouldn't pay me unless I drank something."

"Did you think he was trying to poison you?" she asked excitedly.

"As a matter of fact, the thought did cross my mind. But what reason would he have to kill me?"

"To keep the location of his collection a secret," she ventured.

"If he was going to kill me, then why bother blindfolding me?"

"So you wouldn't get suspicious," she said without hesitation. "If he hadn't blindfolded you, you would have wondered why he didn't, and you might have jumped out of the car when it slowed down for one of those turns you didn't count."

I couldn't help but laugh. "You read too many murder mysteries. Anyway, he obviously didn't poison me."

"Maybe it was a slow-acting poison. Or maybe he put it in one of those time-release capsules. I saw that once in a—"

"He didn't poison me. The beer hadn't been opened. Even so, I smelled it when I opened it and it smelled right, and you know my sense of smell is infallible."

"That's true," she conceded, "but your eyes are failing."

"They're not failing. I just have to use reading glasses sometimes."

"I wonder why our sense of smell doesn't fade like our sight as we get old?"

"I have no idea. Anyway, the beer smelled fine. It tasted right, too. In fact, I wanted to sit there and finish the bottle."

"Even without chips and salsa?"

"Well, there was that," I conceded. "I also wanted to get away from him. He was creepy. So when he called me back to the swinging door, I left the half-full glass of beer on the coffee table. He cracked the door slightly and counted out twenty-five crisp hundred-dollar bills one at a time as he transferred them from his left hand to his right. Then he stuck the money in my shirt pocket and told me to walk over to the door and face the window with the blindfold in my hand. After I'd been standing there for a minute or two, I heard the door open. The driver came up behind me, took the blindfold from my hand and tied it around my eyes. He led me out into the car and drove me home."

"So you never got a look at him?"

"No. My instructions were to be standing in front of my shop at exactly five o'clock facing the Plaza. That's why I missed our cocktail hour yesterday. I was told not to look back, just to keep facing the Plaza. I heard a car drive up. Someone got out but left the motor running. He walked up behind me and said, 'I'm going to blindfold you now.' You know the rest."

"Maybe the driver was the guy at the house."

"Couldn't be. After the driver closed the door with me standing in the entryway, the guy inside told me I could take the blindfold off, and he was standing across the room in the swinging door. There wasn't enough time for the driver to go out through the front door, run around, and come through a back door and be standing there by the swinging door."

"Maybe he closed the door without going through it and then tiptoed quickly over to the swinging door."

Susannah has a vivid imagination.

"I think I would have heard him. And anyway, what would be the point? Why would he not want me to know he was the driver?"

"So you couldn't identify him," she said as if that were obvious.

I stared at her. "But I *can* identify him. I saw him in the house."

"Yeah, but you can't identify him as the *driver*."

I shook my head in confusion. "What difference does that make?"

"I don't know. We'll have to find out what he was up to before we can know that. Maybe being the wheelman makes the crime more serious."

"Wheelman?"

"That's what it's called, Hubie. If he just takes the money, then it's theft. But if he takes the money and also drives the getaway car, then maybe it's something like aggravated theft."

"It wasn't a getaway car, Suze. He was just taking me home."

She shrugged. "He takes you home, takes off the blindfold while you face Mecca or whatever, tells you not to turn around, and drives away, leaving you standing there with twenty-five hundred dollars in your shirt pocket. So why did you say you need to go back to get your money?"

"Because when I reached into my shirt pocket to move the bills from pocket to wallet, they were gone."

"So that's it! He didn't want an appraisal at all. That was just a pretense so he could rob you."

"If so, he must be the stupidest robber in history. The money he took from me was what he gave me to begin with."

"Oh, right. Well, it may not be robbery, but he did gyp you. You didn't get paid for your work."

"Maybe. But it's also possible the driver just saw the opportunity to make a quick twenty-five hundred, and the collector guy doesn't know the driver took my money."

"Unless they're the same person."

"We already went through that. They were not the same person."

"If you'd done that counting the turns thing, you could go back and find out for sure. But it's too late now."

"Not really," I said smugly.

"Oh?"

"Yeah. I know the address."

3

A week before what turned out to be my ill-fated trip in a blindfold, a cadaverous man walked into my shop just before closing time.

My first thought was less than charitable. I was afraid he was going to die or at least pass out and make me late for margaritas with Susannah.

Of course I would have helped him as much as possible, but it did seem a little unfair that I had sat around all day without making a single sale and then just before closing time, some moribund tourist picks my shop to collapse in.

But he didn't collapse. Despite his ashen complexion and skeletal frame, he made his way towards the counter in a hesitant gait, but with a glint in his eye. When he reached it, he put his hand on it for support and said, "Could you get me a chair, Hubert?"

I dragged the one I was using around to the front of the counter and he lowered himself unsteadily into it. I noticed that in addition to being completely bald, he had no eyebrows.

Once he was seated, he looked up at me and said, "You don't remember me, do you?"

"No," I admitted, "but give me a minute, and it'll come to me."

"Same old Hubert. Like a peanut M & M—a hard center of confidence hidden by a thin shell of reticence."

"Now I know who you are. You're the poet laureate of New Mexico."

"Same sense of humor, too," he replied. Then he gave me that half smile, and I knew who he was.

"Mr. Wilkes, welcome back to my shop."

Carl Wilkes is a treasure hunter like me. Well, perhaps not completely like me. I think his list of what one is allowed to do in the pursuit of pots is more inclusive than mine.

"I wasn't sure I'd be welcome after the trouble I caused you."

Wilkes was the guy who convinced me to get the Mogollon water jug that was in the museum at the University.

"It all worked out in the end. And even if it hadn't, you didn't twist my arm."

Now he seemed too weak to twist even his own. He had a thick, close-cropped beard when first we met. He was thin then. Now he was emaciated. The beard had evidently gone the way of the hair and brows.

I knew he wanted something, but we chatted about the museum caper until he finally came round to the purpose of his visit.

"You know a man here in Albuquerque who owns a couple dozen Anasazi pots?" he asked.

"No, but I wish I did." I had thirteen at the time.

"You're not likely to meet him," he replied. "He's a recluse. He's considering selling the pots and wants them appraised."

I nodded but said nothing.

"Would you consider doing it? He'll pay you twenty-five hundred dollars, and it shouldn't take more than an hour or two."

"Why ask me? You can appraise them as well as I can."

Another smile. "I appreciate the vote of confidence, but you know more about ancient pots than anyone. And there's another reason for me not to do it. I'm hoping to serve as agent for the sale, and I'm sure the guy's sharp enough to realize that having the agent appraise the merchandise is a conflict of interest."

"Because the agent might lowball the estimate to make it easier to sell?"

"Yeah, and then take a kick-back from the buyer who got the good deal."

It sounded like something Wilkes had heard about, maybe even done. That started me thinking about the ethics of the situation.

I may be labeled a pot thief by Congress, but I have a code of ethics when it comes to my business which I prefer to think of as treasure hunting. Wilkes said he was "hoping" to serve as the agent for the sale, which implied that he didn't have a firm agreement to do so.

Two dozen Anasazi pots would be worth at least a million dollars. The agent's ten percent would be a hundred thousand, a sum that made the twenty-five hundred appraisal fee look like chump change.

I'm not an immodest fellow, but Wilkes was right about my knowledge of ancient pottery. There aren't too many people who deal in it, none on the scale I do. If the collector asked around, he would hear about me and might decide to ask me to act as his agent. But if Wilkes could convince me to do the appraisal, that would rule me out as the agent.

If the drift of my thinking makes you suspect I didn't completely trust Carl Wilkes, then you followed that drift correctly. The fact that he hadn't mentioned the gentleman's name wasn't merely an oversight on his part.

Don't get me wrong—I like Carl. But as we say in New Mexico, you can like your neighbor, but you still brand your cattle.

I told him I'd think it over.

You already know I decided to do the appraisal because you came in just as I was riding blindfolded to do it. I had come to the conclusion that I couldn't serve as the agent even if the collector asked me to do so. I didn't even know he existed before Carl Wilkes told me about him, and I couldn't steal Carl's potential client even if that client wanted me to. And I stuck with that opinion even though I suspected Carl might steal a client from me if the situation were reversed.

So that's how I ended up taking out my seamstress tape, my sketch pad, and my pastel pencils. Why pencils instead of a camera? Because the owner had specified no photographs. That and I probably couldn't figure out how to work today's digital cameras.

I wanted the sketch pad and pencils so I could draw each pot and its designs. The seamstress tape is flexible, so I could wrap it around the base, widest spot, and rim of each pot to get the dimensions. Using pastel pencils would allow me to put in the right shades. Size, shape, design, and color are four of the key elements used to classify pottery. The other two are the type of clay and the glaze.

You can't be absolutely certain about those last two without lab tests, but I've seen enough pots and thrown enough pots to make reliable guesses, so I wrote down next to each sketch the sort of clay used and the glaze. Then with all that information at hand, I could check my records and the records of other sales and put an accurate price on each piece in the collection. The agreement was that I would send the estimate, listed by piece, to a post office box.

Carl had made an accurate estimate of the time involved, about two hours. That's just for the rough sketches. They didn't need to be any more than that. I wasn't going to frame them. I wasn't even going to stick them on my refrigerator door with magnets. They were just visual notes about what was in front of me.

I finished all the pots to the left of the fireplace in about an hour. The first pot on the top shelf to the right of the fireplace was sufficiently above my 5' 6" that I couldn't put the tape around the pot to measure it, so I had to estimate. Also, I couldn't get close enough to see the detail in the glaze. I could see the potter had used slip, a pigmented clay slurry that stays put during firing and is better than just a thin glaze.

Despite the pot being on the top shelf, the going seemed easier than it had with the previous ones. In fact, my listing of the attributes of this particular pot came so easily and naturally that I found myself writing some of them down before I'd even seen them.

Huh?

I put the sketch pad and pencils down and stared at the pot. I realized I knew what the other side of it looked like even though I couldn't reach up to turn it around and look.

The front side had a sort of swirly fiddlehead design that may have been a symbol for a waterfall or a desert whirlwind. Or maybe it was a symbol for a fiddle. We anthropologists make a lot of assumptions about symbols used by extinct tribes based on scanty evidence, and I suspect we are wrong more often than we are right, but that's the nature of the science.

The back side of the pot had the same design except the potter's stick had slipped in her hand for some reason—maybe one of her kids had bumped into her—and even though you could see where she had tried to coax the slip back into the right curve, she hadn't been able to do so completely and hadn't taken the time to smooth the whole thing down and start over.

Which is what I would do today, but then I'm not working in a cliff dwelling with kids swarming around me and needing to replace a pot one of them carelessly knocked over.

How did I know the design on the back had that little miscue? Because I had put it there. The pot on the top shelf to the right of the fireplace was one of my copies.

4

Segundo Cantú had walked into my shop shortly after Christmas carrying a large cardboard box.

The box didn't sport wrapping paper or ribbon, and Cantú definitely didn't look like Santa Claus.

"I hear you can make copies of pots."

I took an immediate dislike to him, perhaps because he dispensed with any greeting or perhaps because there was something in his tone that implied I was a Xerox machine that did pots.

"Good afternoon," I said.

"Well," he said impatiently, "can you?"

"I can when I want to."

"Good," he said, "I want an exact copy of this one."

He evidently didn't hear the "when I want to" part of my answer.

Cantú was tall and slant-shouldered with long arms. His hatchet face was dominated by a long thin nose, a high forehead, and eyes that constantly darted.

He opened the box and placed the pot on my counter.

It almost took my breath away.

Because of the passage of ARPA, there are very few ancient pots being dug up these days. Even without legal restraints, there wouldn't be many because the things are damned hard to find. I have a knack for knowing where to look honed by years of walking the desert and graduate work in archaeology, but I'm lucky if one in a hundred of my illegal digs turns up anything even close to the pot Cantú placed on my counter.

Pots that were dug up when it was legal to do so are all in museums, private collections, or the inventory of a few lucky merchants like myself. Of course, there's no way to know when a pot was unearthed, so when I do get lucky, I put my find in one of my display cases with a discreet little tented card on which is written a small price.

Small in font size, not small in the quantity of dollars.

If someone questions the provenance of the pot, I tell them I dug it up when it was legal to do so. I suppose some people would see that as lying. I see it as an elliptical way of saying that as far as I'm concerned, it still is and always will be legal to dig up old pots.

It's no different from digging for gold. Except gold is easier to find.

You can see ancient pots in museums or in my shop, but you certainly don't expect a guy like Segundo Cantú to be carrying one around in a cardboard box.

The pot had an odd shape, about fifty percent wider than it was tall with a narrow opening. It had two fiddlehead designs one hundred and eighty degrees apart, one slightly irregular, but you already know about that.

"How much do you want for it?" I asked.

"I want you to make a copy of it," he said, his long arms flopping around nervously.

"You already told me what you want. Now I'm telling you what I want. I want to buy it."

"It's not for sale."

Maybe he wanted a copy so that he could put the original in a vault for safekeeping and put the copy on display. I've heard of women with big diamonds who have zirconium copies made because they don't want to risk wearing the ten-carat original in public.

Maybe the reason it wasn't for sale was because he had already sold it, and he wanted a copy to remember it by. It didn't really matter why he wanted a copy. If he wouldn't sell it to me, I could either make a copy or not. But I hadn't yet given up on buying it.

"I'll give you twenty thousand for it."

He didn't blink and he didn't hesitate. "It's not for sale. You gonna copy it for me or what?"

I quoted him a price of five thousand, a little on the high side because I didn't like him, but not so high—I hoped—as to make him change his mind. I needed the money.

He tried to bargain with me, but I told him the price was firm. He finally agreed. I gave him a receipt acknowledging he'd left the pot with me and a date a couple of weeks ahead when he could return for the copy.

He returned in February with another pot in what appeared to be the same cardboard box. I copied it for him. Then he brought me a third one in early April. All three of those copies I made for Cantú turned out to be in the collection I appraised.

I remembered Cantú's last visit was in April because I was working on my income tax return. I also remembered that he paid me five thousand in cash for each copy.

Even though it was cash, I reported the income on my tax return, maybe because I was abiding the law or maybe because I was afraid Cantú might deduct it as an expense on his tax return and some sharp-penciled IRS agent would see a payment to Hubert Schuze on Cantú's return and then look up my return to see if there was a corresponding income entry.

What a racket income tax is. Cantú gets a deduction. I get higher taxes. The feds get more money to spend trying to put me out of business.

Each time Cantú left a pot to be copied, I had the pleasure of admiring it, going over every inch of it as I created its twin. Seeing the flaw in the first one—the one with the fiddlehead design—made me think about the woman who made it.

My business has a logo displayed in gold leaf on the windows. The logo—initially foisted off on me by Susannah and some art student friends of hers—turned out to be spectacular. Two stylized hands. One reaches up, the other down. Together they form a double helix pot, the hand below the soil surrendering it to the hand above.

But something more is passing between those hands. I named my shop Spirits in Clay.

I know it sounds New Age and corny, but I couldn't think of anything better at the time. Looking at Cantú's first pot made me feel better about the name. There is a spiritual connection between the ancient potter and the modern one who finds her work.

Of course I didn't find this one. It came into my shop in a cardboard box. I didn't own it and probably never would, alas.

As I studied that pot, a thought popped into my mind. I could make two copies and keep one for myself. Or make three—one for Cantú, one to keep, and one to sell.

Then I realized I couldn't do that with a clear conscience without getting Cantú's permission, and I was certain he wouldn't grant it.

My code of ethics again.

I reconciled myself to the fact I'd never own that piece by focusing on the bright side. I'd get to study it and handle it. I might have lived my entire life without seeing it, but now it would be in my possession for fourteen days.

In that regard, it was similar to my love life. I've been fortunate to be involved with a few women whose allure was even greater than ancient pottery, and I never got to keep one of them either.

I wondered briefly if it was sexist to draw an analogy between a woman and an inanimate object. I decided it wasn't because I didn't mean it that way. I continued looking at the pot and thinking about its maker.

The connection between the ancient potter and the contemporary one has nothing to do with tribe or ethnicity. We humans are not our bones, our flesh color, or our eye shape. We are what we *do*. Culture is behavioral, not biological.

One good example is the anthropologist who "goes native," who gets so wrapped up in the culture he's studying that he actually becomes part of it. Permanently. Marries into it, adopts its language, dress, and customs. Burns his trousers and takes to wearing turtle shells on his knees.

I have a list of beliefs I call Schuze's Anthropological Premises, abbreviated SAP, which is what some of my cynical friends say you have to be to believe them.

SAP number 1 is that any human being can practice any culture. If a Norwegian newborn were adopted by a couple in the Acoma Pueblo, that child would grow up to be exactly like all other Acoma children. He would look a bit out of place, but everything about him other than his blue eyes and fair skin would be pure Native American.

He would not someday suddenly long for herring. He would not dream of being a ski jumper in the Olympics.

He might someday wonder why he looked different. If his adoptive parents told him about his origins, it is possible that curiosity might drive him to Norway to learn about his roots. He might even decide to become Norwegian, to give up the culture of his upbringing and learn the culture of his biological parents.

He could do that. Remember that SAP 1 says any human being can practice any culture. But he would have to *learn* to be Norwegian. It wouldn't just spring forth from his DNA. It would be as difficult for him to learn to speak Norwegian as it would be for you to learn to speak it.

Many people today don't understand this. They adopt babies from China, bring them to the United States, put them in our public schools, and raise them like you would raise any other child in America.

All well and good.

Then they decide to give them Chinese lessons. Now learning another language is always a good thing. But why Chinese? Spanish would be more helpful here in America. Arabic is growing in importance. Italian is beautiful.

Just because a child is of Chinese ethnicity does not mean she has to learn Chinese. Your culture and your language are determined by who raises you and where they do it, not by your genes.

In the interest of full disclosure, I should mention that several years after I earned my business degree, I was kicked out of the anthropology graduate program at the University of New Mexico. You may want to take my opinions with several grains of salt.

If you suffer from hypertension, I recommend a salt substitute.

5

After I surprised susannah by telling her I knew the address where I'd appraised the pots, she decided the explanation of that would probably take us through another round of drinks, so she summoned Angie for refills.

After delivery, I took a sip to make sure they were as good as the last ones. They were.

"I discovered something surprising during my appraisal. Three of the pots in that collection are copies I made."

"You sold the collector three copies? How come you didn't recognize him?"

"I don't think the guy I saw there was the collector."

"Then who was he?"

"I have no idea, but I think the collection actually belongs to a guy named Segundo Cantú."

"What kind of name is Segundo?"

"It's the kind that comes after Primero and before Tercero."

"You're kidding, right?"

"No. It's not too common these days, but some Hispanic families used to name their male children after the order of their birth."

"What, they couldn't think of any names so they just went with numbers?"

"Ordinal numbers."

"Huh?"

"When people say numbers, they normally mean cardinal numbers—one, two, three, like that. I was just pointing out that the names are ordinal numbers—first, second, third."

She gave me that impatient look she always gives me when I say anything about math. "What difference does it make what sort of numbers they are? It's still weird."

"I don't know. Look at all the kings and queens with numbers. Elizabeth the First, Henry the Eighth—"

"I rest my case. No one is weirder than the royals."

"Good point," I replied and hesitated. "I've forgotten what we were talking about."

"Segundo Cantú."

"Oh, right. Well, he brought me a pot last December and paid me five thousand dollars to make a copy of it."

"Why would he want a copy of his own pot?"

"Let's come back to that. He came back again in February with a second pot he wanted copied. Then he brought a third one in April."

Susannah recited the order of months out loud while sticking up a finger for each one. "December, January, February, March, April."

She studied her fingers. "He was bringing you a pot every other month." She paused briefly to think then said, "You should get the fourth one this month."

"Somehow I don't think I will. So let's get back to your question of why he was having me copy his pots. Here's my theory. He decided to sell his collection. But before he sold a pot, he wanted a copy of it. So he sold the first pot in December, telling the buyer he could take delivery in a few weeks. Meanwhile, he has me copy it. After he gets the copy, he gives the original to the buyer and collects his money, let's say fifty thousand."

"So he pays five thousand for the copy and sells the original for fifty? He's coming out way ahead."

"Right. Then in two months, he sells another one, and we go through the same rigmarole. Same again two months after that. But then some buyer offers to buy the whole collection. Cantú agrees. That's why he wanted the whole collection appraised. So I'm not going to get any more copying business from him."

"Why not? If he wanted copies when he was selling them one at a time, why wouldn't he still want copies when he's selling them all at once?"

"My guess is the buyer isn't willing to wait that long. It takes me at least two weeks to make a good copy. Multiply that times the twenty-two remaining originals, and you get forty four weeks."

"That's almost a year."

"Yeah, and my experience with collectors is they like owning things, not waiting for things."

"So your copying income has dried up."

"It looks that way. And if I can't get more money for copying Cantú's pots, I at least want to get my twenty-five hundred for the appraisal."

"You still haven't told me why Cantú would want copies of the pots he was selling."

"I don't know. Maybe he needed money but hated the idea of losing his collection so he had copies made as a compromise."

I scooped some salsa onto a chip and ate it. What could be better than Dos Hermanas on a hot summer day, the cool breeze from the evaporative cooler, the soothing sounds of Spanish from the kitchen, the fresh salsa with its jalapeño snap, perfect margaritas, and the best friend a guy ever had sitting across the table.

Frowning. "There's another possibility," she said, her big eyes narrowing in suspicion. "Maybe Cantú was selling the copies and keeping the originals."

"He couldn't have sold the copies. They're still in the collection."

"How do you know they're the copies and not the originals?"

"A fair question. No matter how carefully you copy, there are always little differences. Suppose the original had a black band around it and the band on the copy was slightly wider. Well, that wouldn't mean anything to the casual observer because no two old pots are ever the same. The Anasazi weren't working at Royal Doulton with production lines and quality control. Each pot was a fresh creation. They might use the same design, but they had no way of making two pots identical, so the black band could be wide on one pot and a bit narrower on the next. The person who makes a copy knows when he doesn't get it quite right, and he knows how he erred. So if the copier made the band slightly wider and he's looking at the copy and the original next to each other, *he* knows that the wide-banded one is his copy. But no one else could know that because the copier could have just as easily have made the band narrower."

"Okay, that makes sense. But how do you know the collection you appraised belongs to Cantú? Maybe Cantú was just an errand boy for the collector."

"I guess it's possible," I admitted, "but it seems unlikely. Ancient pots are fragile. I can't see a collector letting some errand boy walk around with one in a cardboard box."

"Then who was the guy there when you did the appraisal?"

"Maybe he was a friend Cantú asked to stand in for him because he didn't want to be there when I came for the appraisal."

"Why wouldn't he want to be there?"

I shrugged. "He's a weird guy. Maybe he thought I might get angry that he was planning to sell my copies as part of the collection."

She got that excited look she gets when she tries to morph reality into a murder mystery. "Maybe it was Cantú in disguise!"

I started laughing. I explained that the guy at the appraisal was older and shorter than Cantú.

"But you said he was stooped over. It could have been Cantú just pretending to be a hunchback."

"What about the older part?"

"Makeup."

"I don't know, Suze. That sounds like a lot of work for nothing. Instead of disguising himself and walking around bent over, why not just get a friend to deal with me?" And then I joked, "If Cantú was going to put on theater makeup, why not take the opportunity to make himself better looking?"

"Good point. From your description, he sounds like the sort of guy I always get on blind dates."

"You don't go on blind dates."

"Now you know why," she quipped. Then she hesitated for a minute and said, "Although I did go on one last night. Well, it wasn't really a blind date, more like an arranged meeting disguised to look like a chance encounter."

"Huh?"

"Some of the students wanted to grab a bite after class, and they asked me to go. I said I was too tired, but they insisted. When we got to the café, there was a guy who seemed to be waiting for us, an international student. He was by himself and there were five of us, two couples and me. They all quickly grabbed seats in such a way that the only empty one was next to Chris. So I figure it was a setup. But no one had said anything to me, and I get the impression they hadn't said anything to him either, so neither one of us had that awful feeling of being on a blind date."

"Chris is the name of a foreign student? Where's he from, Canada?"

"Italy. His real name is Christoforo Churgelli, but everyone just calls him Chris. Seems like a nice guy. Sort of odd, but in a nice way. How did we get on this topic?"

"I have no idea."

She puzzled for a moment. "Oh, right, Cantú not making himself up to be better looking. I still don't see how you can be certain it's Cantú's collection. Maybe he sold the whole thing to the guy you saw, copies and all."

"Could be. That would really gall me because that would mean that weasel sold my copies as originals. He may have made ten times more on my copies than I got for making them."

"And when you sell a pot that you got for free by digging it up, how much more do you make than the person who made the pot in the first place?"

"That's different."

"How?"

"The potters who made the pots I sell are dead. I couldn't give them a commission on the sale even if I wanted to."

"Well, Hubie," she said after draining the last of her margarita, "I know you think the collection belongs to Cantú, but there's only one way you can be certain about that."

6

Which is why I was riding blindfolded again the next afternoon, this time in the passenger seat of Susannah's purple 1995 Ford Crown Victoria.

It didn't start out purple. The factory color was blue, but too many years under the New Mexico sun oxidized the paint in some peculiar way that made it turn purple.

The Crown Vic came with every electronic gadget available— air, power windows, cruise control, power seats, even a power trunk release. None of those things still function.

I doubt she misses the cruise control and how difficult is it to open the trunk with a key? But not having air conditioning in Albuquerque is bad. Having inoperable windows is even worse. So when the little motors that operate the windows burned out, Susannah took the inside door panels off and manually lowered the windows. Of course there isn't a crank, so there's no way to raise them again.

No problem. It rarely rains here and no one is going to steal the car.

I like riding in Susannah's car even though my feet don't touch the floor if I sit all the way back in the seat. You could park a Corolla in there.

Segundo Cantú was listed at 183 Titanium Trail, a street in a subdivision of condos called *Casitas del Bosque*. The other street in the development was named Platinum Place.

In the real Albuquerque—as opposed to its faux southwestern-style suburbs—there are original streets named Lead, Copper, and Silver. All those things are mined in New Mexico. So far as I know, there is no platinum ore in the State. I don't even know if titanium comes from ore, but I don't think we have any.

Susannah mapped out the route to 183 Titanium Trail and insisted I wear a blindfold while she drove there. I protested at first on the grounds that I could just close my eyes and imagine that I was recreating my first trip. But I eventually gave in to her argument that we needed to recreate the conditions of the first trip as faithfully as possible.

I also gave in because she thought it would be "peachy" to have a blindfolded passenger.

She told me to take some time to put myself in the right frame of mind, to imagine I was taking the same trip. When I said I had done that, she set off. We rode in silence as agreed, and I paid attention to how long we went straight, how often we turned and the direction.

Since we had nothing else to go on, we decided she would drive at the speed limit. The ride seemed to match the way it felt the first time except for the fact that the Crown Vic has loose steering and feels like a boat in high swells when you round a corner.

When she came to a stop and cut the engine, I took off the blindfold.

"Well?" she asked.

"Well, I have to admit you were right. Having the blindfold on helped me compare it to the original trip."

"And did it seem the same?"

"I have no idea. The blindfold kept me thinking about *piñatas*."

She took a swipe at me, but the front seat is so big that I just leaned towards the window and she missed.

"It did seem like the same ride," I said after I stopped laughing at her.

"Does the house look the same?"

I fell for it. I actually looked at the house as if I might recognize it. I gave her a look to acknowledge that she got me back for the *piñata* remark. Then I looked at the place in earnest.

The *casitas* were in clusters of six, each one identical from the outside except for the wrought iron numbers on the plank doors. The clusters were low-slung with buttresses at both sides and differentiated by the shade of the stucco—light brown, dusty rose, grey, dark brown, and an awful mustard.

Unit 183 was in one of the light brown clusters. Despite the development's name being *Casitas del Bosque*, there were very few trees around the *casitas* unless you count a few straggly junipers.

There was an irrigation canal at the end of Titanium where it intersected with Platinum. I wondered what sort of alloy those two would create.

On the narrow strip of dirt between the curb and the canal grew a stand of cottonwoods, willows, and catalpas. Maybe they were the *bosque*.

"I need to see inside," I observed rather redundantly.

41

"Go knock on the door and see if anyone's home."

"Are you crazy? What if Cantú answers the door?"

"Tell him you came to see his pot collection."

"What if he doesn't want me to see it?"

She sighed. "It doesn't matter, Hubie. All you're trying to do is get a peek inside. As soon as he opens the door, you'll know if it's where you did the appraisal."

"I already know it's where I did the appraisal."

"Come on. You can't be absolutely certain."

She was right. I didn't know exactly how I was going to get my twenty-five hundred back, but it was pay for appraising the collection, and until I was positive who owned the collection, I didn't know how to go about reclaiming it.

"Let's drive around back," she said and started the engine. We were headed due north. I'd like to claim I knew that because of my Y chromosome, but the truth is I knew we were headed north because the Sandia Mountains were on our right. At the end of Titanium Trail, we turned east toward the mountains onto a service drive. After about a hundred feet, the service drive made a second right angle turn to the right so that we were now headed south and were directly behind the units.

I remembered the window with the cream-colored shade and told Susannah about it as she swung into the service drive. There were one-car garage doors at the back of each unit. She drove slowly along as we looked at each window.

Spotting the cream-colored shade would have strengthened my conviction that this was where the pots were. We spotted it alright.

There was one in every window.

"I can't believe everyone in the neighborhood bought the same shades," I said.

"They didn't. Those are probably the ones that came with the places."

"And no one decided they wanted a different color or maybe Venetian blinds?"

She shrugged. "It doesn't look like the sort of neighborhood where people hire interior decorators."

There was something forlorn about the place. No window boxes, no brightly painted doors, no landscaping.

One of the garage doors opened a few units behind us and a car backed out and headed in our direction. Since the rear service drive was wide enough only for one car, Susannah drove around in front to let the car exit.

Then she said, "Let's look in the garage."

She paid no attention to my protest as she noted Cantú's unit aloud. "Fifth one from the end," she said as she again drove to the back of the units.

She stopped directly behind number 183, got out of the car and peered through the small windows in the garage door as I scrunched down in the seat trying to make myself invisible.

"There's a Cadillac convertible in there," she said.

"That seems a bit fancy for this neighborhood."

"The thing actually has fins."

"Sounds like something Cantú would drive. He's got this boney frame and—"

"Yeah, you told me that. So you think this is the house where you did the appraisal?"

"Of course. It's Cantú's address, it seems the right distance from Old Town, and the house is about the right size. It was roughly twenty-five feet from the entry where I took off the blindfold to the window with the shade pulled down, and these *casitas* are about that deep. On top of all that, I did notice how far my blindfolded walk was from the car to the front door, and this front sidewalk is the right distance. Everything fits."

"So now what?"

"He's probably here since there's a car in the garage. Maybe I should keep checking back until I find the garage empty and then see if I can get in somehow."

"Break in like you did at Berdal's apartment?" she asked mischievously.

"I didn't break in. You kicked in the door."

"You were *trying* to break in, but you weren't very good at it. Meanwhile, I was standing out there freezing my butt off, so I finally just kicked the door in because we'd still be standing there if I hadn't."

And the banter continued in this mode as we drove back to Old Town. At one point I put the blindfold back on surreptitiously. When Susannah finally noticed, she almost ran off the road laughing. It was almost five, and I was looking forward to discussing how to reclaim my missing appraisal fee with Susannah at Dos Hermanas.

Then I remembered she'd told me she had a date that night with Chris the foreign student. Since it was Friday, that meant I wouldn't see her again until Monday at five, at which time she would probably tell me her date had been a disaster.

She's unlucky in love, but it never gets her down. Still, I worry about her. I resisted the temptation to warn her about Italian men, partly because it was not my place to do so, but mainly because I don't know anything about Italian men.

What I did know was that 183 Titanium Trail had to be the

house where I did the appraisal. The location seemed right. The size seemed right. The back window was in the right place. The door was the right distance from the curb. It was Cantú's address. I was positive it was Cantú's collection.

But I had a nagging feeling in the back of my mind that some small detail was wrong.

7

Martin Seepu was standing in front of my shop with a pot in his hand when Susannah dropped me off.

I said, "I hope your uncle's not in dire need of money, because I can't afford to buy that pot right now."

"That's what these tourists have been telling me all afternoon."

"They don't even know your uncle."

"I meant the 'can't afford to buy that pot' part." He shook his head in mock disgust. "There was a time in this country when white people had money."

Martin's uncle is a gifted potter who occasionally sends Martin to me with a pot he wants to sell. His works are traditional for his pueblo, which is why I buy them.

I don't like contemporary adaptations and experiments. New Mexico's potters are free to use iridescent glazes and decorate their pots with embedded casino chips if they want to, but I don't have to buy and sell the stuff.

Another reason I buy Martin's uncle's works is they always sell within a few months. Some people know quality when they see it. The only reason his pots don't bring even more is he isn't famous. He could be if he promoted himself or allowed an agent to do so. A book about him or a TV special would quadruple what he can get for a pot, but he doesn't want that.

Martin respects that. So do I, but I grimace when someone walks off with one his pots for three or four thousand even after I mark it up.

"So you've been taking advantage of my absence to hawk your wares on my doorstep?" I asked.

"You can see how well that worked. I did get one offer. A fat kid offered to trade his ice cream cone for my pot."

"Probably figured he could snooker an Indian."

"I have to admit I was tempted. An ice cream would have tasted good on a hot day like this. But he'd already licked it."

"I don't have any ice cream, but I do have some cold beer."

"You got Tecate?"

"You gonna turn me down if I don't have the right brand?"

"A man's got to have standards."

We went through the store to my living area in the back. While Martin pulled a couple of Tecates from the fridge along with a bowl of salsa, I looked up Cantú's number and dialed it. A recorded voice told me the number was no longer in service, as if it had been discharged from the military.

I dumped chips into a bowl, and we took everything out to my patio, a ten by fifteen space on the east side of my building surrounded by an eight-foot adobe wall. The building shades the patio in the afternoon, so the air was already twenty degrees cooler than the noon high of ninety. The twin cottonwoods swayed ever so slightly, their leaves alternating between lime green and silver.

I tutored Martin in math when he was a kid and I was an undergraduate. I think the aim of the program that oversaw placing university students in the pueblos was for us to function something like the Big Brothers program. Martin already had a big brother and a big sister as well. He also had two parents who provided him all the guidance he needed and more than he wanted. So I taught him math just to feel like I was doing something useful.

He evidently harbors no grudge about that because he comes to visit me frequently.

I told Martin about Segundo Cantú. He listened attentively with that blank expression he wears. After I finished, he took another sip of his beer. He likes it straight from the can. I always pour mine into a glass.

After a few minutes, he said, "People who collect old pots are strange."

"Including me?"

"Especially you. Of course you got some reason to do it—this trading post."

I chuckled at him calling my shop a trading post, but I guess it is in a way.

"My people believe the four elements are earth, air, fire, and water."

"Just like the ancient Greeks," I noted.

"We made a little progress since them. We divide each of those into four subcategories." The leaves rustled and he tilted his head skyward.

"And those subcategories are?"

"The four kinds of earth are sand, clay, rock, and another word that I guess would translate as soil. It's what you can grow things in." He ate a chip—no salsa—and sipped some beer.

"I just know there's a reason you're telling me this."

"There are also four types of clay," he continued. "My uncle taught me. White clay, changing clay, shrinking clay, and hot-fire clay. Even though you're a yellow-haired devil, you probably know this stuff."

"Correction. I'm a brown-haired devil."

"Yellow-haired has a better ring to it."

"It does," I agreed. "The white clay is kaolin, no doubt about that one. The changing clay is probably what we call fire clay because its plasticity can change like crazy. Shrinking clay would be ball clay because that shrinks a lot during firing, and hot-fire clay is probably plain old earthenware clay because it requires a high temperature to fire properly, although so does kaolin. Why are we talking about this?"

"I'm making a point about pot collectors."

"I think I missed it."

"That's because I haven't made it yet."

"Ah," I said and drank some Tecate.

"Pot collectors don't know anything about clay. They don't know about firing. They don't know the true meanings of the designs. Why do they want the pots?"

"Because as Shelly said, 'A thing of beauty is a joy forever.'"

"That was Keats," he corrected.

"I was just testing you."

"I don't think they collect pots because they're beautiful. I think they collect them because they're rare."

"I agree. The rarer, the better. Look at the most desired collectibles of all time—the 1943 copper penny, the 1918 stamp with the plane upside down—the thing they have in common is not their beauty or historical significance or anything like that. It's just that they are rare."

"One of those 'inverted jenny' stamps sold for half a million a couple of years ago," he noted.

"So you're saying that pot collectors are weird because they buy pots just because there aren't many of them to be bought."

"I guess the same could be said of all collectors."

It was right after he made that statement that the dog fell out of the sky.

8

The next morning I drove down the South Valley along old Highway 85, avoiding the Interstate. Friday had been a scorcher, but I'd slept with a light blanket. The dry air cools quickly when the sun goes down, and you feel the effects of being a mile above sea level.

I wore chinos and a hyphenated shirt—light-yellow, button-down and long-sleeved. The sky was cerulean blue, lit indirectly by the sun, which had not yet cleared the Sandia Mountains. I lowered the windows and the Bronco filled with the scent of alfalfa.

I turned west on an unnamed dirt road alongside an irrigation canal lined with cottonwoods and followed it to the modest adobe that Emilio and Consuela Sanchez call home.

It's like home to me as well. Consuela was my nanny, arriving at the tender age of sixteen when I was born. My mother was a wonderful woman who never quite felt at home in what she regarded as the rather untamed wilderness to which her husband had brought her shortly after their marriage. But she used to say you have to "bloom where you're planted," and she set about improving Albuquerque by organizing garden clubs, civic beautification drives, and ladies auxiliaries.

What the ladies were auxiliary to I never knew.

She taught me by word and deed the meaning of decorum and propriety. Despite her sober upbringing and somewhat rigid values, she was a warm and affectionate person, but it was Consuela who attended to the small things in the life of a boy that contribute mightily to the man he becomes.

She was an older sister and a second mother. She taught me Spanish the old-fashioned way, by talking to me in that tongue from the day I came home from the hospital. My mother taught her to make dishes like *Boeuf en Croute* and leg of lamb with mint sauce.

But when Mom wasn't home, Consuela fed me *caldillo*, *chile con carne*, *pozole*, and *sopaipillas*. For vegetables we had *frijoles*, *flan de maiz mezclado*, and *verdolagas* that she gathered wild. Her cooking molded my palate. I'm as likely today to go to a French or Japanese restaurant as I am to take up skateboarding.

We left my parents' home the same year, she to get married, me to enroll as a freshman at the University.

Emilio changed Consuela's name from Saenz to Sanchez. A year later they had Ninfa who turned out to be an only child like me. When Ninfa married and moved to California, it broke her mother's heart. Consuela has lived since with two hopes, that Ninfa will give them a grandchild and that she will come back to live in New Mexico.

Emilio came to the United States in 1953, twelve years old but concealing his youth in order to enter the *Bracero* Program.

"I walked all day from San Diego de Alcalá to Chihuahua," he told me years ago. "I was surprised when I arrived, *amigo*. There were more people at the Trocadero than in my village."

"What was the Trocadero?"

"I don't know from where comes this word, but it was a building near the railroad station. There I stood in line with the others to see the Americans who would choose those to become *Braceros*."

He was sitting that day, as he always does, with his back perfectly straight, his shoulders squared, his head held high. Working for fifty years with a short-handled hoe gave him sinewy muscles and leathery skin, but it never broke his spirit nor bowed his head.

"How did they choose?"

"First you have . . . How do you say *entrevista*?"

"Interview."

"Yes. First, you have the interview with one of the gringos." He looked at me and smiled. "If he like what you tell him, he send you to a second American. He takes your hand and rubs it to see if you have worked. I feel embarrassed by this gringo holding my hand, but everyone must do the same, so I do it. They like what I say and they like my hands because I work hard in my village, so I get a paper. The third gringo say for me to make my *equis* on the card, but I tell him I know how to write, and I write my name very carefully on the card. I am very proud to have this card."

"What happened after you got the card? How did you get to the U.S.?"

"The next day, we ride in a cattle train to Ciudad Juarez. There we wait in a park for two days until the *migras* sign our papers. Then we walk across the bridge to El Paso. I remember, Huberto, when I show my card to the American on the El Paso side. He smile at me and move his arm to tell me keep walking. I think in my head that America let me come in, and it was the happiest day of my life."

He paused for a moment. "The Americans in the Trocadero never smile. But I always remember that guard on the bridge. After passing the bridge, they put us in the back of farm trucks and take us to a large building in a small village in New Mexico called Hatch. There they spray white powder on us to kill lice. I know I have no lice, but I say nothing. I just close my mouth and eyes and hold my nose because the spray is strong. They give us *chile con carne* to eat, and we sleep on the ground."

"The next morning the farmers come and choose which of us they want. I am surprised because some of them are Mexican, and I think in my head that America must surely be heaven where someone from Mexico may own a farm. I do not know that these men who look like me and speak Spanish are not from Mexico. I was a young and foolish boy, and I think I will work hard and save my money, and I will buy a farm in Hatch and marry an American woman."

"And you did all those things," I pointed out in admiration.

"Yes, Consuela is American, and so I am also as her husband. And we both work hard and buy together this small piece of land and build this house with our hands. But it is not a farm."

"You grow everything you need."

"Consuela has the green thumb."

"And you are here instead of Hatch, and perhaps that is also good."

"Yes, because we are close to you and our other friends."

He sat for a moment in reverie. "The first man I work for in Hatch is not a Mexican. He is a gringo. I never know his name. We call him only *Patrón*. I pick chiles for one dollar for each one hundred pounds. I make almost twenty dollars the first week, and I think I will become rich. But the picking is not the only work. I must also do the irrigation at night, and for this I do not receive money. I ask the other *Braceros* if I must say something to the *Patrón*, and they tell me to say nothing, for if I make a complaint, I will be sent back to Mexico, and perhaps they will be sent back as well. So I work both day and night six days each week."

"On Saturday after work, we can go to the store. The other *Braceros* buy cigarettes, but I save my money. On Sunday we go to mass, and some Sundays we do not work after mass. We play baseball and make *barbacoa*. The *Patrón* is a very cold man, but he pay me each week, and when I return to Mexico, I have almost five hundred American dollars, more than my father make in his life."

I thought about that story as I saw Emilio come around from the back of the house, a wide grin on his face. He removed his sweat-stained hat and gave me a strong *abrazo*.

"Welcome, amigo. I hope you have brought a large hunger, for there is much to eat."

"I could smell your *barbacoa* all the way from Albuquerque. It's pork today."

He laughed and his dark eyes smiled. "Consuela always say you have the best nose. But let us not stand here alone and thirsty. Come, come."

We circled to the back where a dozen of his neighbors had gathered, and he introduced me to two I didn't know, a nephew and niece of the Calderon family who own the land on which Emilio and Consuela's house sits.

At least according to the records in the Bernalillo County Courthouse. In fact, Emilio and Consuela bought the small plot many years ago, but county ordinances prohibit subdividing land in this area, so no legal transfer can take place.

It doesn't matter. In this small community, agreements among neighbors are more binding than papers in a courthouse.

Jesús Calderon stood over a fifty five gallon steel barrel that had been cut in half and made into a *barilla*. There were twenty pounds of charcoal under the grate and fifty pounds of meat on top. The smoke made my empty stomach churn with anticipation,

Jesús gave me an *abrazo* as I stepped close to admire his handiwork. Manny Chapa put one hand on my shoulder and slipped me a cold can of Tecate with the other. I offered up a small prayer of thanks for being born in New Mexico.

9

I arrived home around four, bloated with beer and *barbacoa*.

My plan for a late afternoon *siesta* was foiled by the arrival of Miss Gladys Claiborne on my doorstep. Gladys, whose name has been prefixed throughout her life by "Miss" even during the forty years of her marriage, owns and operates the eponymous Miss Gladys' Gift Shop two doors down from me.

She is well known in Old Town for her hand-sewn line of tea cozies, placemats, aprons, handkerchiefs, and dishtowels, most bearing the image of either San Felipe de Neri Catholic Church or the colorful Gazebo in the center of the Plaza.

She is also well known for her casseroles, each of which is an intriguing and often startling mixture of things that are themselves ready-to-eat foods such as canned tuna, Campbell's soup, and crushed crackers. Other lighter versions rely on Jell-O, miniature marshmallows, canned fruit, and cream cheese.

Since the death of her husband, she has no one to feed these concoctions to, and I seem to have drawn the short straw. You already know how my tastes run in food, so you will understand my desire to tactfully avoid her cooking.

Especially when I've just eaten several pounds of pork and drunk a quart or two of beer.

But to my surprise and relief, she came not to feed but to introduce.

His name was T. Morgan Fister, a distinguished looking clean-shaven gentleman with silver hair, light blue eyes, and a strong chin.

Mr. Fister wore brown linen slacks over a pair of woven leather loafers. His maize cotton shirt had a spread collar, monogrammed on the left with the letters TFM. I thought the monogramist had made a mistake in ordering the letters until I realized the middle letter was slightly larger, indicating, I suppose, Mr. Fister's family name having pride of place in the little pantheon of letters on his collar. Monogrammed clothes are an affectation.

Over the expensive shirt, he wore a herringbone jacket with a leather patch, not on the elbow, but on the right shoulder where the stock of a shotgun would be braced while the man in the jacket blasted doves out of the air for sport. I think those are called hunting jackets.

He had an easy smile and a firm grip, and he seemed genuinely happy to meet me. He said nothing about himself, being a true gentleman, but made me instead the center of attention, asking me questions as if I were the most interesting chap he had met since his last bird-killing sortie with Prince Charles.

No, he wasn't English. He just seemed like the sort who would hunt with Charles. I'll say this for Fister—at least his ears were of normal proportion.

When I redirected my gaze from T. Morgan to Miss Gladys,

she was looking up at her new friend, enthralled. Oh my God, I thought—she's in love.

"You'll never guess where Morgan is from," she said, and she gave me a look that indicated I should try nonetheless.

He also fell silent, obviously not wanting to spoil her fun. They both looked at me in anticipation.

"Winchester," I said, a wild guess that stemmed from my thinking about the guns. And by the longest of shots, I actually got it right. There's evidently a town in Virginia by that name and Fister came from it.

"Heavens to Betsy," declared Miss Gladys, "However did you know that?"

T. Morgan tried to maintain his calm demeanor as a look of apprehension spread across his face.

"Have we met?" he asked cautiously.

"Of course," I said, "just a few seconds ago."

He gave a brief nervous laugh. "But have we met *before*? You do look familiar."

I try never to be a bad person, but mischief is in my nature, and now that he was off balance, I intended to press my advantage and see where it led.

"What brings you from Winchester to Albuquerque?" I asked, not answering his question.

"I have an interest in Native American artifacts."

"And he's also here to tend to his aging mother," Gladys volunteered.

I turned to him. "Where in Albuquerque does she live?"

"Oh," he said, "she's back in Virginia. I'll bring her out as soon as I've located suitable quarters for her. By train of course. She dislikes air travel."

"Goodness," said Gladys, "I was under the impression she was already here."

"No doubt my fault," he said without hesitation. "I'm so anxious to see her here that I speak as if it's a *fait accompli*."

Gladys giggled. It was disgusting. Then she said, "Morgan's speech is just peppered with those cute French phrases. I do think it sounds so high class, don't you agree?"

"Using French is quite *de rigueur* these days," I said.

"Yes," he said uncertainly.

"One might almost say it's *derriere*," I added.

"Precisely," said Morgan.

"I must tell you, Morgan, that Mr. Schuze is the most talked about man in Old Town," said Gladys. "He keeps the most irregular hours at his shop, and he has been arrested several times, all of which turned out to be mistakes by the police."

At this news, Fister broke into a contented smile that seemed to say he had met a fellow traveler, a scoundrel like himself, someone who would keep his secret safe for fear of having his own misdeeds uncovered.

But whereas I only appear to be a scoundrel, I was convinced that T. Morgan Fister was the real thing.

"So," he said with a note of triumph in his voice, "What is the mysterious business you engage in when your shop is closed and no one knows your whereabouts?"

I looked at them both in turn with a grave expression. "Do not breathe a word of this. What I do in my other life is undercover investigations for the police."

I watched all the blood drain from Fister's face.

10

Stuffed shirts from Benjamin Franklin to William James have preached the importance of habit and routine to the well-led life. Early to bed, early to rise. Plan ahead. Show up on time. Make lists. Keep a calendar. Never put off until tomorrow what you can do today.

Steven Covey has written eight books on habits. Not how to get *rid* of them, how to *cultivate* them. And those books are best sellers. It's a sad commentary on America's literacy that a book urging you to adopt the habits of "successful" people—meaning those who wear dark suits, lack a sense of humor, invent things like hedge funds and send their kids to Harvard—is a best seller.

Habits are hogwash. A million years of evolution prepared us to be flexible, to live life in the order it comes. No anthropologist has ever found evidence that cavemen had ulcers. They ate when they were hungry, slept when they were tired. They probably didn't think about it much, but they knew a truth we've forgotten. Life is what happens to you while you're busy making other plans.

Routine dulls the intellect and crushes creativity.

Some things, of course, require planning. But most of them—invasions, political campaigns, cruises, football matches—are better left undone in the first place.

All of which is to say that it was out of character for me to be awake and on the road at 5:30 on a Monday morning. I drove to Titanium Trail, went around to the back of Unit 183, and peered into the garage. I figured there was little chance of anyone spotting me at that hour of the morning.

I don't know why we refer to such hours as "barbaric." Civilized men are much more likely abroad at five in the morning than are barbarians.

The Cadillac was in the garage. I drove around to the front and parked on the shoulder about fifty yards from unit 183. I adjusted my rear-view mirror so I could see the front door just in case anyone came out that way, but what I was really watching for the was the Cadillac.

I was on a stakeout.

Okay, I admit I had done a little planning. I had a thermos of coffee and a book about Einstein that Martin had urged me to read. When I donned my reading glasses, the print was crisp and clear. The same could not be said of the subject matter.

The coffee and the book fought each other, the book trying to put me to sleep and the coffee trying to keep me awake. After a while, the book seemed to be winning.

I stopped reading. I stared into the mirror. Nothing happened. After another while, I looked into the passenger-side mirror and saw a van parked on the opposite side of the street. I didn't remember seeing it when I had first turned onto Titanium Trail. I hadn't noticed it arrive. Perhaps it came up while I was reading. But there it was, a white van with "United Plumbing" in big black letters.

I stayed until around ten. A quick scan of the van as I drove by on my way home revealed the driver and passenger seats to be unoccupied. There may have been someone in the back of the van—there were no windows back there—but I assumed it more likely held pipes, fittings, and tools.

I was back the next day at eleven in the morning, figuring that if I showed up at a variety of times, I might catch someone leaving or coming back. The United Plumbing van was where it had been the day before. I drove around to the back, found the Cadillac in the garage, drove around in front, put the glasses on, and read page five of the book on Einstein.

When that hour was up, I ate three tacos filled with caramelized jalapeños and some of the barbecued pork Emilio had sent home with me on Saturday. I drank a Tecate I'd brought along in a small cooler filled with ice. I wanted more, but I didn't want a DUI on my record. I knew one beer wouldn't put me over the limit.

Even though it was only one beer, it eventually worked its way through my bloodstream and kidneys and then into my bladder. I made it until just after two before going home.

I was back at midnight, driving slowly down the service road with my lights off. I stopped, peeked into the garage and saw the Cadillac by the light of the moon. I was beginning to think I understood why the phone was no longer in service.

The next day, Wednesday, I showed up at three in the afternoon and stayed until after six. The Caddy was in the garage. I wanted to go in and try to start it up. I suspected it was inoperable, just being stored there.

The United Plumbing van showed up about four thirty while I was trying to read. It sat there for about five minutes, then turned and left. A skinny brown arm jutted out from the driver's side.

Nothing unusual about a brown arm in Albuquerque. Half the population is Hispanic with varying shades of brown skin. The other half of the population, be their ancestors from France or Lithuania, are just as brown because we all get baked by the sun year around.

The driver had a ponytail that stuck out under a baseball cap. I tried to get a look at his face, but couldn't focus. Then I realized I still had the reading glasses on. By the time I took them off, he was gone.

Maybe he realized he forgot a piece of pipe he needed. Or maybe he wasn't really a plumber. Or maybe I was slightly paranoid.

As I left, I made a resolution to come back one more time.

11

"Wouldn't it have been easier just to knock on the door instead of wasting all that time on a stakeout?"

"It wasn't wasted," I corrected her. "I used the time to read about Einstein and the uncertainty principle."

"I thought the uncertainty principle came from Heisenberg."

"It did. But Einstein rejected uncertainty."

"You could have done the same by just walking up and knocking on the door."

She's relentless. "That's what you would do," I said. "You have that rancher mentality—saddle up and ride. I'm more the wary type. And anyway, the captain's seats in the Bronco are big and comfortable and a great place to read."

"Then why did you only get to page five?"

"That was the subject matter, not the environment. Martin insists I should read this book, but it's taking me about an hour a page." I shrugged. "Maybe once I get my head around the basic ideas, the rest of it will be easier."

"What are the basic ideas?"

"Well, the uncertainty principle has to do with the behavior of subatomic particles, things like electrons and protons. Apparently those particles behave very differently from everyday objects like rocks and rutabagas."

"Rutabagas? The book said that?"

"No, that was just my example."

"That's a strange example, Hubie."

"Okay, forget the rutabagas. Just think of a rock. If you throw a rock, the path it takes is determined by the direction you throw it and how hard you throw it. If you're good at throwing rocks, you can even make a sort of intuitive calculation and hit something you aim at."

"So?"

"Well, subatomic particles evidently don't work like that. If you throw one, you have no idea where it might go."

"I don't think you can throw an electron, Hubert."

"I know that. What the book is trying to do, I think, is contrast the predictability of the path of a rock and the path of an electron. Or a tennis ball. That's a better example. You've seen those machines they use to shoot tennis balls at you so you can practice?"

She nodded.

"Well, you can aim them, and I assume you can set the speed, so if you want to practice returning hard serves with your backhand, you crank up the speed and aim the thing to your right."

"Only because you're left handed. Most people would aim it to their left."

"Whatever. The point is that once you have it aimed, it isn't suddenly going to shoot a ball straight up in the air or into the net. Where the ball goes is predictable."

"And where an electron goes isn't?"

"Exactly. They have things called electron guns that shoot out a stream of electrons, but where each one goes is unpredictable. That's why they call it the uncertainty principle."

"Other than teeny little subatomic people playing tennis with electrons, why should anyone care about this?"

I shrugged. "Intellectual curiosity."

I could see she'd heard enough, and I'd already said everything I knew about it, so she told me about her date with Chris Churgelli. They had attended a poetry reading at the University. After it was over, they walked to a coffee place on Harvard where they met some other people who had been at the reading.

In case you're wondering, there are also streets in that neighborhood named Columbia, Dartmouth and Yale. I guess the founders of my *alma mater* wanted it to have some connection, however tenuous, with prestigious eastern schools.

"So you drank coffee and talked about the poetry?"

"That's what Chris and the others did. I just sat there staring at him."

"Handsome, huh?"

"Beyond belief. A face like Michelangelo's *David*, skin the color of almond biscotti, hair with the luster of Tuscan leather, eyes the color of Pinot grigio grapes—"

"He has red eyes?"

"Pinot grigio grapes are green, Hubert."

"Oh."

"Anyway, he's a pleasure to look at and a pleasure to listen to."

"He knows a lot about poetry?"

"I have no idea. I didn't understand a word he said."

"A really thick accent, huh?"

"Not really. He has just enough of an accent to sound romantically European. And a great vocabulary. He knows a lot more words in English than I do."

"Then why couldn't you understand him?"

"Because he uses words in funny ways. Not in a wrong way, exactly. Just . . . oddly."

"Like?"

"Well, he described one line of a poem as 'Fragrant with intentionality.'"

"Sounds like typical academic jargon to me."

"Here's a better example. He didn't like one of the poems because it was 'Fulminating in a wide arc.'"

"I see what you mean. But how is he in normal conversation when you're not talking about poetry?"

"About the same. He said we should eat at La Hacienda—we're going there this Friday—and when I asked him why La Hacienda, he said he heard it was, 'A luminary for its fabrication of local repasts.'"

I started laughing.

"It's not funny, Hubert. This is a seriously handsome guy, and he seems to be a nice person, too. He's a gentleman, he looks at me when I talk to him, he never brags or does all the other stupid things men do. But I don't know if I can maintain a relationship with someone who speaks a different brand of English."

She sat there thinking for a minute. I took advantage of the lull in conversation to wolf down several chips loaded with salsa. Then she said, "You think I should say something to him?"

I hate it when she asks for advice regarding her love life. I feel like I'll be responsible if something goes wrong. Which it usually does.

"How long has he been in the States?"

"He entered in the spring semester, so I guess about six months."

"Maybe he was even worse when he first arrived. If he spends more time talking to you, maybe he'll come to realize his English is not colloquial, and he'll improve."

"I like the part about him spending more time with me," she said, as if I were advocating it.

"So," I suggested, "I wouldn't try to correct his English at this point unless he asks for help. Of course if it doesn't improve in time, then maybe—"

"Oh, it'll improve. I'm sure of it. Thanks, Hubie. I can always depend on you for good advice."

And I got that sinking feeling, so I changed the subject.

"Miss Gladys has a beau."

She shook her head slightly. "I know. She brought the scoundrel to lunch at *La Placita*."

"So you think he's a scoundrel, too."

"It's obvious. The first piece of evidence is his name—T. Morgan Fister. Never trust anyone who uses a middle name that way."

"I know lots of people who use their middle name, and most of them are perfectly normal and nice."

"Name one."

"Well, one of my high school friends was named Bascomb Ronald Harvey. Bascomb was his grandfather's name. He was stuck with it on his birth certificate, but he always just went by Ronnie Harvey."

"Not the same. If he had called himself B. Ronald Harvey, he would have been a different person and not nice."

"Hmm." I tried to think of people I knew or knew about who had that sort of name.

"You may have a point," I conceded, "because the first person I thought of with a name like that is J. Edgar Hoover."

"There's also G. Gordon Liddy," she said.

"And E. Howard Hunt."

"And W. Clement Stone who financed those two burglars."

"Scary," I said.

"And J. Danforth Quayle," she added.

"That's the best example. Notice how all of them are in politics?"

"Writers do it too," she said, "like F. Scott Fitzgerald."

"Or W. Somerset Maugham."

"And don't forget Swami Kriyananda," she said.

"I can't forget him because I never heard of him in the first place. And how does he fit into this conversation?"

"Because his birth name was J. Donald Walters and he's a writer."

"On what?"

"Yoga, I think."

"Politicians, writers and swamis—all charlatans."

"F. Scott Fitzgerald wasn't a charlatan."

"You're right. And his first name was Francis, so who came blame him for not wanting to use it."

"He could have just gone by Scott Fitzgerald," she pointed out.

I had no reply to that, so I asked her what her second reason was for thinking T. Morgan was a scoundrel.

"He left me a tip that was way too large."

"That's bad?"

"Here's how it works. Ten percent is about normal in New Mexico. Sometimes you get only five percent but usually that's because the person doesn't know any better, not because they're cheap. And some people follow the fifteen percent rule. When a woman leaves you a big tip—over twenty percent—it's usually because she can't do the math or simply isn't paying attention because money isn't that important to her. But when a man leaves a really big tip, he's trying to impress whoever he's with or he plans on hitting on you."

"How do you know the big tippers are planning to hit on you?"

"It's not hard to figure out, especially when they leave a phone number on the check or a duplicate of their motel room key."

"You can't be serious."

"Sometimes they put the money in your hand and try to cop a feel at the same time."

"Geez, how do you stand it?"

"It doesn't happen that often. Usually you can spot them in advance, so when I pick up the check of a weirdo who's been leering at me, I take the coffee refill carafe along, and if he gets too close, I accidentally on purpose spill hot coffee into his crotch."

Susannah is a woman with gumption.

12

My nephew Tristan lives in a student ghetto on Gold, just a few blocks from the University where he studies—of all things—computer science. It's hard to imagine we sprung from the same gene pool.

He doesn't look like me either. I'm short and compact with straight brown hair trimmed short and combed close to the scalp. He's tall and slightly pudgy with black hair that hangs down in loose ringlets. He also has olive skin and what the girls think of as bedroom eyes. He's a genuine person, and girls like that even better.

He's not really my nephew. He's the grandson of my Aunt Beatrice, but I call him my nephew and he calls me Uncle Hubert. He supports himself with periodic gifts from his Uncle Hubert and by doing odd jobs having to do with computers. One particular task he is often paid for is called de-bugging. It doesn't involve insects, but that's all I know about it.

Given that I'm on the wrong side of forty-five and live alone in the back of my shop, Tristan is as close to a son as I'm ever likely to have. I enjoy his company. I also turn to him for help when technology intrudes itself into my life, and it was for both those reasons that I dropped by his apartment.

I waited until I thought he was awake—noon—and came with a gift of tacos filled with the last of Emilio's *barbacoa*. No jalapeños in this case. Tristan doesn't share my taste for *comida picosa*.

I also had my laptop with me because he had told me to bring it when I had called about the current matter. You may be surprised that I have a laptop.

So am I. Tristan gave it to me because I had some security issues in the store. He hooked up a camera that takes a picture when anyone enters. The picture goes to the laptop where it is displayed by some black magic along with the time of day when the person entered. All of which is triggered by a laser beam across the door.

Theoretically, I could use the laptop for all sorts of other techie stuff like swamping the internet, playing games, and sending email, but I'm not interested in those things.

Tristan was eating the tacos and drinking something called a Jolt Cola, which he said used to advertise itself as having "all the sugar and twice the caffeine." He would probably have preferred a beer but he told me he had class that afternoon.

"You never take morning classes," I noted.

"Interferes with my circadian rhythm," he said.

"And all that caffeine doesn't?"

"Nah, it just gets me going."

"When I was a student here," I began and could already see his eyes rolling back in their sockets, "most of the required courses were in the morning."

He smiled at me. "I think you may have mentioned that before. But now everything you need is offered in the afternoons."

"I guess the faculty finally gave in to the sleeping habits of students," I lamented.

"Actually," he corrected, "it's the faculty who drive the schedule. They refuse to teach early classes."

I was preparing a biting remark about the faculty when I remembered that I often eat breakfast at ten in the morning with my shop closed and dark.

He finished the tacos and wiped his mouth with the sleeve of his sweatshirt, saw me see him, and said, "I'm doing laundry today."

"I suppose you need some quarters?"

He allowed as how he did, and I gave him four hundred of them in the form of a single bill with Benjamin Franklin on it. I noticed that Ben's picture is now off to one side, the bill has weird pastel colors added to the traditional green, and a metallic strip runs through it.

The Federal Government—they made my profession illegal, tax me when I continue to do it, and now they have nothing better to do than tinker with our money.

Tristan handed me the device I had come for. It looked like a middle-school science project, a perforated metal plate about six inches square with wires and little devices all stuck together. One wire dangled down the side and had a sort of plug thing, but not the sort that would go in a wall outlet.

"You made this?"

"Yep. Sorry it looks so messy, but you just need it for one use. I'm not going to market them."

"Could you?"

"Not and stay out of jail. Let me show you how to use it. You plug this into a USB on your laptop," he said, indicating the wire hanging from the device. Then he handed me a small plastic device the shape and size of a piece of gum. "You put this into a different USB." He showed me the USB slots in the back of the laptop. "Then you just aim this at the garage door and push this button. You'll have to hold it down for a while depending on how long it takes to find the code. When you see the garage door start to open, you can let go of the button, but not before. Otherwise, you'd have to start over."

"I won't need electricity to make this thing work?"

"The battery in the laptop will supply the current. Make sure it's charged up."

"So I'm using the computer just as a battery?"

"No, the jump drive has a micro in it that will direct the device to run through all the possible codes in sequence."

I asked him what a jump drive was and he pointed to the gum-sized piece of plastic.

"How long will it take?"

"Given when the houses at *Casitas del Bosque* was built, they probably have second generation garage door openers. Those are coded by setting DIP switches in the transmitter and the receiver to a matching combination. Depending on the number of switches, there can be up to two hundred and fifty-six codes."

"So the most switches they have is eight."

"Uncle Hubert! How did you know that?"

"I don't know what a DIP switch is, but I recognize two hundred and fifty-six as the eighth power of two, so if the switches have two positions, off and on, and there are eight of them, then the number of combinations is two raised to the eighth power, and that's two hundred and fifty-six."

He was staring at me in admiration. It felt good but was fleeting.

"Anyway," he continued, "It can run through a signal every second, so the worst case would be about four and a half minutes."

I should have left it there, but I had to ask. "Why are they called second generation?"

He laughed. Not at me, but because he thought the history of garage door openers had a funny chapter.

"The first garage door openers sent an unencoded signal. That was fine when they were a novelty. But the FCC limits their frequency to between 300 and 400 megahertz, so after a lot of them were installed, it would sometimes happen that two people in the same neighborhood would buy units that turned out to be sending on the same frequency, and when you pressed your opener, your door went up but so did the guy's down the block."

"What's megahertz, a super car rental company?"

He likes it when I make jokes about technical terms.

After a polite laugh, he said, "So they put codes in them that you set with DIP switches. But anyone with a few diodes and resisters and a soldering iron can make a device like this, so after a few burglaries, they came up with the third generation openers that have more complicated coding."

His eyes lit up. "And now there's a new model that works by reading your fingerprint. You just put the tip of your finger over the opener and up goes the door. I'd love to have one of those. Of course, I'd need to get a garage first."

Then he looked at me and said, "Do I want to know why you need this?"

"I'm not going to steal a car from a garage," I pledged. "Let's just leave it at that."

13

I drove from Tristan's apartment directly to 183 Titanium Trail.

Where, contrary to my nature, I walked boldly up to the front door and rang the bell.

Or at least pushed the button. I didn't hear a bell. I put my ear to the door and my finger to the button and still heard nothing. I looked at the door and wished it was one of those with a little window. I could look inside, see the pot collection on the left wall and know that Segundo Cantú was the guy I needed to see concerning my twenty-five hundred dollars.

Maybe I'd also hit him up for another hundred and thirty thousand, which is what I calculated he would have cleared if he sold my copies as part of the collection.

I got back in the Bronco and drove around back. I inserted the jump drive into the computer. It didn't jump, but tech terms make no sense. I attached Tristan's widget to the computer and pushed the button. In less than a minute, the door shuddered slightly and then moved. Dust flew up from where the door had rested against the floor.

I walked into the garage and put my hand on the hood of the Cadillac to see if the engine was warm. I don't know why I did that, exactly. I'd seen it in an old movie, and it just seemed like something I should do.

The hood was cold to the touch.

The door from the garage into the house was locked.

I said a bad word.

Then I remembered something I read in one of Susannah's murder mysteries, one where the hero was a burglar of all things, an expert at picking locks using a collection of little odd-shaped pieces of steel. The process requires placing several of those in the keyhole and then manipulating them until you get each of the tumblers to move. I guess what you really do is make the little picks line up in such a way that they mimic the bumps on a key.

I didn't plan on trying that—way too complicated for me.

But the burglar also mentioned something called "loiding a lock," which is called that because you use a thin strip of celluloid. You just stick the celluloid into the doorframe and it slides around the bolt, forcing it out of the bolt hole.

Loiding won't work on a deadbolt. You have to pick those. But it will work on simple locks where the bolt is held in the hole by just a spring. And where the door doesn't fit in the frame too tightly because you need to have room to force the celluloid around the bolt.

I pulled on the knob and the door moved at least a quarter of an inch. There was ample space between the door and the jamb. I thought I could break in.

Loiding doesn't require skill, but it does require celluloid. Or you can use a credit card. I had neither with me. My driver's license would probably work, but I didn't want to risk damaging it. "No officer, I didn't try to alter my license. It just looks that way because I used it to break into a house."

I went back to the Bronco and found the service card that came with it, a little piece of plastic just like a credit card that I used when the Bronco was in warranty. I thought about how long ago that was, wondered where the years had gone, put that thought aside and realized I had no use for the warranty card.

Other than loiding the door, which it did perfectly. But not until I had closed the garage door because loiding locks is an activity best done out of anyone's sight.

The door led into a kitchen. There was a swinging door against the back wall just where it should have been. I pushed it open. The window with the shade was where I remembered it. The beige carpet was still on the floor but dirtier than I remembered it.

It was the same room.

But the coffee table was gone. And the Danish modern couch was gone.

I turned around to look at the fireplace. It was still there. Those things are the devil to pack up and move.

The shelves were there too. They were still running from floor to ceiling, nice deep shelves just perfect for displaying a collection of old and valuable Anasazi pots. A collection, say, like the one that had three of my copies in it.

Except the copies were not there. Which didn't surprise me, because neither were any of the other pots.

14

"So he sold the collection, packed up his belongings, disconnected his phone service, and moved."

"That's the way it looks," I said. "But he didn't clean up like you're supposed to when you move out. The carpet definitely needed shampooing."

"So you'll never see the twenty-five hundred," she lamented.

"Probably not," I agreed. "Unless I can find out where he moved to."

"Carl said he was a recluse. He wouldn't leave a forwarding address."

She was probably right. I took a sip of my margarita. It didn't have quite the zip it normally does, but that was the fault of my mood, not the bartender.

"If you can't find Cantú," she suggested, "maybe you can find the driver and he could tell you where Cantú went."

"How can I find the driver? I never saw him."

"But you heard his voice."

I started to say you couldn't identify someone by voice alone, but of course you can. I would recognize Susannah's voice in an instant. But could I recognize the driver's voice?

"His voice was vaguely familiar," I said, "but maybe it just sounded like a typical voice. He didn't have a lisp or a stutter or anything like that."

"There's no such thing as a typical voice. Think back. Did he speak clearly or slur his words? Did he have a regional accent? Did he make his A's long or short? What about pitch? Baritone, tenor?"

I closed my eyes and tried to recall the few things he had said to me. "Well, he sort of clipped his words like maybe he was nervous. He may have been Hispanic. He made his "O"s round, if that makes sense to you."

"See, you can tell more than you think about voices."

"I guess you're right. But even if I could recognize his voice, how would I go about finding someone based on their voice?"

"Easy," she said. "You place a want-ad for a driver and then listen to the voices of people who call about the job."

Susannah is always quick with an answer and enthusiastic in offering it.

"Wait a minute!" she said. "He didn't take the Cadillac."

"Probably couldn't get it started. The thing looks like it's been there for years. Did I tell you the hood was cold?"

She shook her head in consternation. "I still don't understand why you did that. But forget about whether it runs. It has to be registered, and when it comes up for renewal, he'll have to give his new address to the Department of Motor Vehicles."

"And I'll do what, walk in to the DMV and ask to see all registrations in the name of Segundo Cantú?"

"Hmm. What if you just kept an eye on the car? He has to come get it eventually, doesn't he?"

"Sure. I could go there every day and watch for the next few weeks or months. It would take me that long to finish Martin's book anyway."

"You're joking, right?"

"Not about how long it would take me to finish the book. But I'm not interested in another stakeout. Look, he probably got a million for the collection. He can afford to just abandon a beat-up old car."

"It's not beat-up. It's just old. Actually, it's a classic, a 1969 Deville convertible. One as sharp as that one is probably worth at least ten thousand dollars."

"How do you know that?"

"I like cars, remember?"

It amuses me that Susannah knows about cars and football and I know about cooking and making clay housewares. So much for gender stereotyping. It just illustrates SAP number eight: environment and upbringing determine your personality more strongly than does your gender.

"Maybe you could sell the car to get your money"

"I don't think you can sell a car unless you have the title."

I had been ready to forget the whole episode even before walking into Dos Hermanas, but Susannah's questioning forced me to keep thinking about it, and even though some of her suggestions seemed weird, she had once again—as she frequently does—led me finally to a fruitful thought.

"But you don't need the title to drive it. I could drive it away and park it somewhere. Then I could leave a note for Cantú telling him I have his car and to contact me."

"Yeah. You could hold the car for ransom."

I hadn't thought of it in those terms, but she was right.

Then she turned serious and said, "What if it's not Cantú's house?"

"I was in it today, remember? It's the same house."

"But what if he just rented? What if the car belongs to the landlord, or anyone else for that matter?"

"This is too complicated," I said, sliding back to my original opinion—forget the whole mess and move on.

"Not really. All we have to do is check the registration."

"We?"

"Sure," she said, draining her glass, "partners in crime. Your car or mine?"

So I finished my drink and handed Angie cash for the tab and a tip. It was fifteen percent and not a penny more. Wouldn't want her thinking I was hitting on her. On the other hand, she does have those dark, deep-set eyes and those . . . never mind.

We took Susannah's Crown Vic to 183 Titanium Trail where I used Tristan's device for a second time.

I didn't have to loid anything this time because we didn't need to get into the house, just into the car, specifically the glove compartment, where we found a current vehicle registration in the name of Segundo Cantú.

"Okay," she said. "You're right. It is his house. And it's his car and you're going to hold it until he pays you."

"But I can't drive it away. I don't have the key."

"You don't need a key." She took out her pocketknife and slid down under the steering wheel. The next thing I heard was the starter motor, and after a few turns the thing coughed and wheezed and stuttered. Then it actually started and ran.

"How did you do that?"

"I just hotwired it."

"Huh?"

"It's easy. You just cut the wires to the ignition switch and thread them together. These old cars don't have all the fancy interlocks where you can't move the steering wheel without the key, so they're a snap to hotwire."

"And you learned this where, reform school?"

"On the ranch. When a switch went bad on a tractor or backhoe, we didn't have time to drive a hundred miles to a parts place, so we just hotwired them."

I felt uneasy because I'd told Tristan I wasn't going to use his device to steal a car. "So now we're into carjacking?"

"You don't know much about crime for a burglar. You can't carjack a vehicle unless the driver is in it. You're just keeping it safe until he comes back for it."

I felt a little better. "And until he pays me my twenty-five hundred."

"That, too," she said and gave me one of her great big smiles.

"What if he never comes back?" I asked her, feeling the need to check out this scheme to see if it made any sense.

"Then you still have the car. Maybe there's some rule about abandoned cars, like you can say he left it with you, and you don't know where he is. And if he fails to renew the registration, you apply to be the new owner."

It made sense. Cars must occasionally get abandoned, and the State must have some way of dealing with that.

"What if Cantú comes back, finds the note, and instead of calling me, calls the police and reports the car stolen? I could be arrested for grand theft auto."

She solved the car theft issue by leaving a note for Cantú that read, "Dear Mr. Cantú. Your car has been moved to a safe location. To retrieve it, place an ad in the personals section of the *Albuquerque Journal* with the message, "Wanted, Titanium Cadillac", and a phone number where you can be reached."

Very clever, I thought. If he did report it stolen, there was no way to connect it with us.

15

You're probably still wondering about the dog that fell from the sky.

What actually happened was the dog, a wretched creature that had probably been abandoned, was being chased by a pack of teenagers. They had seen him enter the alley behind my store and had split up, some running in from the west end and some from the east. When the dog saw them coming from both directions, he had clambered onto the roof of my Bronco, which I keep parked in the alley and then jumped over my patio wall. The lower limbs of one of the cottonwoods had slowed his fall but also spun him in an odd way so that he sort of tumbled to the ground, landing awkwardly and then springing up with a menacing growl.

I learned all this after the fact. Except for the falling part. I saw that in person. Father Groaz had seen the boys and was hot on their trail. When they saw the dog go over my wall, they gave up the chase and were just leaving the alley when the big priest confronted them.

The good Father is 6' 4", weighs in at around 240 and has a bushy black beard and penetrating Rasputin eyes. His accent alone—think Bela Lugosi with a bass tremolo—would scare most people. Put that voice in a bear of a man in a black robe, and sinners are suddenly clambering for the straight and narrow.

He gave the boys a good scolding, took down their names, and told them if they weren't in mass on Sunday, he would visit them and their parents. They all attended, including the one who was a Methodist.

When the dog descended into my patio, I thought he was rabid. His eyes were full of fear and his growl full of menace. But Martin calmly extended an arm downward and made a long shushing noise, whereupon the animal fell silent and dropped down on his belly. Martin continued with the sound and the pointing, and the dog eventually got up and walked over to Martin who started rubbing him behind the ears.

"What are you, some sort of dog whisperer?"

"Native people know how communicate with animal world," he said in his Jay Silverheels voice.

"Native man with pony tail full of dog poop," I responded.

"True, but I'll bet Hollywood would buy it."

Looking at the critter at Martin's feet, I could almost understand why someone would have abandoned him. He looked like a cross between a collie, a chow, and an anteater. The anteater part would have explained the extremely long neck that sagged down from his shoulders and sort of swayed to and fro as he walked. The droopy neck gave him an obsequious look highlighted by big sad eyes.

The chow in him explained the thick auburn coat while the collie accounted for the longish snout and a tail that—unlike the turned-up version on a chow—slanted down at an angle matching that of the neck. The tail had longer finer hair than the body, and that made it seem as large as his neck, the end result of which was that if you saw his profile in the dark, you couldn't tell front from back.

I had left Martin with his new friend and gone out to the alley where I caught the tail end of the confrontation between Father Groaz and the miscreants and also heard the full story after the boys were allowed to leave. We chatted for a minute before I returned and told Martin what had happened.

"He know where the animal came from?" Martin asked.

"No, he'd never seen him before."

"What you gonna do with him?"

I looked at the dog sitting obediently in front of Martin. "I'm not going to do anything with him. He's your dog."

Martin put his left hand under the dog's chin and turned the animal's gaze in my direction. He pointed at me with his other hand and said, "Go over there, boy."

Whereupon the accursed cur did exactly that, walking over to me and plopping down at my feet.

"Now he's yours," Martin said, rather triumphantly I thought.

I tried to send him back to Martin, but each time he took a step in that direction, Martin would just hold up a palm and the dog would stay by me.

It was too late in the evening to call the no-kill shelter, and I didn't want to call animal control because I didn't know what they might do.

"I guess I'll keep him here tonight and take him to the shelter in the morning," I said.

"Right," said Martin. There was a smug note in his voice I didn't like.

After Martin left, I rolled a pork loin in cumin and coriander and threw it in a very hot frying pan with a thin coat of corn oil. After I had a nice crust all the way around, I pulled the pork out with tongs. Incidentally, never use a fork for such a task. Piercing meat while it's cooking allows the juices to escape. I put the meat in a pie pan and slid it into the oven to finish.

I uncorked a bottle of Gruet *Blanc de Noir*, New Mexico's finest champagne, and poured some in the hot frying pan to deglaze it, stirring up all the little browned bits until they were absorbed in the liquid. I took the pan off the fire and added a little honey and cream and a big handful of cilantro.

I had some cooked black beans in the fridge. I took those out and put them in a saucepan to warm. I removed the meat from the oven, poured the juices that had come off it into the sauce and set the pork aside to rest. Then I retrieved a champagne flute from the freezer and filled it with Gruet.

I put half the pork in a bowl and took it out to the patio. The dog sniffed at it and then looked up at me with those sad eyes.

"It's all you're going to get tonight," I said to him, "so take it or leave it."

16

On Monday morning I took the dog shopping. He picked out a bowl and a collar. He didn't want the bandana, but I bought it anyway.

I thought the bandana might make his neck appear less elongated.

We rode in my new Cadillac. I wanted to put the top down but couldn't figure out how to do it. But it was fun to drive even with the top up, and I was feeling pretty smug when I drove back into Old Town until I saw Whit Fletcher down the street in an unmarked police car.

"You keep funny hours for a merchant, Hubert," he said in greeting as he walked over from the car and met me at my door.

"My business is based on high mark-up," I replied, "not volume."

"We both know your business is based on selling illegal pots, and you probably do that at night, but the shop makes a nice front. Anyway, it's none of my concern. I got enough to worry about what with murderers on the loose. Speaking of which, Hubert, I need you to do a favor for me."

Whit and I are friends. After a fashion. We've known each other a long time. He doesn't care about my illegal digging, and he's helped me get out of a couple of jams when I was the suspect in a murder. Of course he's also the one that made me the suspect, but I don't think he ever thought I was guilty. He knows I'm a pacifist.

I've also helped him out financially. Not bribes. I wouldn't offer that and he wouldn't take it. But if there's money to be made on the side and no one gets hurt, he's always interested. So I figured this was another deal like that. Something, for example, where I would claim a reward because he wasn't eligible to receive it because of him being a policeman and then we'd split the money. I was totally unprepared for what he wanted.

"What I need," he said, brushing his always-in-need-of-a-haircut silver hair off his forehead with a big meaty hand, "is for you to identify a body."

A shiver ran down my spine, or up my spine or whichever way it is they run.

"A dead body?"

He gave me one of his patient looks. "If it was a live one, Hubert, we wouldn't need you to identify it. We could just ask it who it is."

"I don't know, Whit. I'm kind of squeamish, and the idea of looking at a dead body . . . Well, I'm not sure I could do that."

"You never been to a funeral? This here's the same thing 'cept the stiff's in a metal drawer instead of a casket. We slide it open, you tell us who it is. Takes ten seconds."

"But why me?"

"We think you might know the deceased."

"Why?"

"Police business. Nothing you need to know."

"But surely someone else could do it. I'm sure I don't know who it is. Even if it *is* someone I know, I can't be the only person who knew him. I'll bet there's not a single guy on the planet who is known only by me."

"What makes you think it's a guy?"

"Why, is it a woman?"

"Why don't you just come along and see?"

While I was thinking about it, he said, "You got a license for that animal?"

"He's a dog," I said.

"That a fact?" He sounded dubious.

"Do I need a license?"

"I have no idea. I guess I could check the ordinances." Then he said, "You get a new car?" He had seen me drive up in the Caddy.

"It belongs to an acquaintance of mine."

I didn't want to go to the morgue. I didn't care whether the dead person was a man or a woman. I didn't even care if it was someone I knew. That sounds callous, but that's not the way I mean it. If it was someone I knew, then I'd find out eventually through the usual means, and I'd feel sad. But I couldn't help the dearly departed by telling the police who it was. Couldn't they check fingerprints or something? Why involve me?

But failing to cooperate with a Detective First Grade of the Albuquerque Police Department is not prudent, especially considering that he was intimating he might poke into the issue of my new dog and my new car.

In Whit's car on the way to the morgue, I practiced glancing. I would imagine Whit as the dead guy. I'd stare straight ahead and then on the silent count of three, I'd glance at him and then look away as fast as possible. Then I'd ask myself if I had seen enough to make an ID. I wanted to do it so fast that the image of the dead person wouldn't be burned indelibly into my memory. But I didn't want to do it so fast that I couldn't make an ID and would have to do it over again. That's why I was practicing. I tried it several different times.

Finally, Whit asked, "You got a crick in your neck or something?"

"Just a nervous tick," I answered.

Then I sat quietly and tried to imagine who I might know who might now be dead.

The room with the metal drawers was bigger than I had imagined. A lot of people die in a city the size of Albuquerque, but unless you know one of them, you never think about it.

At least I don't. I've been told there are people who read the obituaries every day. I suppose they have a reason for doing that, but I don't think it's a reason I would understand.

It's bad enough finding out someone I know has died without finding it out by seeing his or her name at the top of an obit: "Lucretia Melendez, 1964 – 2011."

"God, I went to high school with her!" I would utter aloud as I choked on my morning coffee.

Not really. I don't know anybody named Lucretia Melendez. But if I did and she died, I'd much prefer for someone to call me and say, "I have some sad news about Lucretia . . ." And if no one thinks to call, then I probably wasn't close enough to her to be deeply affected by her passing.

Why am I running on about this? Oh, right, I was thinking about who might be dead.

Well, they slid the drawer open like Whit said. I made the quick glance I had practiced for.

And it worked. It was so quick that I barely had the chance to react. I didn't become nauseous. I didn't get light-headed. In fact, the two feelings I had were relief that the task was over and surprise that I recognized the face.

Not the whole face. Mainly the forehead. Especially that supra-orbital ridge.

The guy in the drawer was the one who had been in Cantú's house and had counted into my hand the twenty-five hundred dollars that I was now trying to recover by holding a Cadillac for ransom.

It came to me that it was probably the dead guy's car, the one I rode to the appraisal in with a blindfold on, and that's why Cantú hadn't taken it with him along with the coffee table, the Danish modern couch, his twenty-two Anasazi pots and my three copies which I was still angry about.

Then I remembered that Susannah and I had seen the registration of the Cadillac and it did belong to Cantú.

Okay, I knew who owned the car. But who was the dead guy? And more troubling, how in the name of all the stars and planets did the police know I could ID him?

As all these thoughts were running through my mind, I heard a faint voice in the background. Then I realized it was Whit.

"Sorry," I said, "Could you repeat that?"

"It's a simple question, Hubert, especially considerin' you and me are standing here in the morgue. Can you tell me the stiff's name?"

I looked him straight in the eye. Whit that is, not the stiff. "I have absolutely no idea."

He stared at me. "You don't know his name?"

"Nope."

"You sure? Because I thought I saw a little glimmer of recognition when you glanced down there."

"Probably just a little glimmer of happiness that the task was over."

"Why don't you take another look, make sure you can't ID the guy."

I turned my head in the direction of the body and then back at Whit. "Sorry. I definitely have no idea what his name is."

"Try it again, Hubert. And this time keep your eyes open."

So I looked again, thinking that this image was going to be stuck in my brain despite my best efforts to avoid it.

But once again it wasn't as bad as I had anticipated. All that practice had paid off. And since I already knew it was the guy in the house, I didn't have to pay attention the second time.

I had to keep my eyes open of course because Whit was watching. But I had something to focus on. I looked at that forehead with as much tunnel vision as I could muster.

And that's all I saw.

I didn't even see his eyes right below the forehead, much less his mouth or what he was wearing. Well, now that I think about it, he was wearing a sheet. I guess I did notice that. And his eyes were closed. I guess I noticed that too. And I think his mouth was closed, but I'm not sure because . . . I'm not going to talk about this anymore because the image of the dead guy is reforming in my brain and I don't want it there.

But I did look a second time, and then I took a deep breath, tried to sound disappointed about my inability to help, and told Whit I was absolutely certain I didn't know the name of the deceased.

17

"I've never been in a morgue. What's it look like?"

"Just like in the movies. There's a couple of rooms with big glass windows where you can see a steel table and a bunch of stuff like scalpels you'd see in a hospital operating room, except I don't think they're as careful about how they make the incisions."

"Yuk."

"Exactly. Then there's the room with the metal drawers that hold the bodies. It's very cold in there."

"Probably a good thing."

It was the evening after I'd visited the morgue, and the first question Susannah asked when I got to Dos Hermanas was what Whit Fletcher had wanted.

We were on our first round, and I could see her thinking about what I'd told her. I expected her thinking would lead to the same question mine had.

"Why did they ask you to make the ID?"

"That's what I've been trying to figure out. So far, I've come up with only two possibilities."

"Wait, don't tell me. Let me guess." She thought briefly and then said, "The driver told them you were there?"

"That's one."

"So all you have to do is find the driver."

"We've already been over that. There's no way to find him."

"Or her."

"It was a him. He spoke to me, remember?"

"It could have been a woman impersonating a man's voice."

"Okay, there's still no way to find *her*."

She thought some more. "The second possibility is the police thought you knew him because of his connection to pots."

"Two for two. But how would the police know he had a connection with pots?"

"They saw the collection in his house."

"The collection is gone."

"Oh, right. Hmm. Maybe there were some more pots in another room."

"No. Before I started the appraisal, I asked if there were any pots other than the ones on the shelves, and he said no."

"Maybe he lied or maybe there were some other pots that weren't part of the collection. Did you search the whole house when you burglarized it?" She asked with a smile.

"I didn't burglarize it. I just went in to make sure it was the right house. If I'd known there was going to be a murder, maybe I would've looked around. But I don't think it would've done any good. The other rooms are no doubt just as empty as the living room."

She loves murder mysteries. I've read a couple only because she urged me to. I didn't particularly enjoy them. But what I enjoy even less is being *in* one.

I guess I shouldn't complain. In all other respects I have a great life. I'm healthy, I have good friends, I love my work and I'm footloose and fancy-free. Well, at least I'm footloose. I didn't know what fancy-free means, so I had looked it up in my *Oxford English Dictionary* that very day. Unlike a paperback murder mystery, the *Oxford English Dictionary* is great to have around the house. In addition to containing definitions for about half a million words, it is also useful in New Mexico for holding the door shut on a windy day.

Susannah interrupted my musings. "I've got it! You weren't alone. There was someone else in the house you didn't see. Let's call him The Third Man. That's the title of a famous Carol Reed film. After the murder, The Third Man told the police you were there."

"Then why wouldn't the police have The Third Man ID the body? They would know for certain that he could do it if he'd been in the house with the dead guy."

"Maybe they did."

"Then why ask me?"

"See, Hubie, this is why you should read murder mysteries. If you did, you'd know why they asked you."

"But if The Third Man had already identified—"

"Even *after* the police know the identity of a body, they sometimes ask other people to identify it in order to see how they react."

"Why would they do that?" I asked naively.

"Because those people are suspects."

"Thanks for telling me that," I said as I felt my stomach knot up.

"I'm just trying to help. If you are a suspect, it's better for you to know so you can be prepared and not let the police trip you up."

"Why should I be a suspect?"

She shrugged in a fashion that was rather too nonchalant in my opinion. "You've been a suspect before."

I started to complain that there was no reason for the police to suspect me, but then that had been true in the others cases as well, hadn't it? But surely it couldn't be happening again. I decided not to worry about it. I was confident there was no Third Man.

"Let's forget The Third Man," I said and waved to Angie.

After our fresh drinks came, Susannah said, "Okay, I'll change the subject. What did you do about the dog?"

"I fed him before I came over here," I said evasively.

It had been almost a week since he'd dropped in on me, and my ad in the lost dog section of the newspaper had resulted in only two calls, both from functional illiterates. Despite the excellent description of the dog I put in the ad, the first person who called was looking for a lost dachshund.

The second call came from a woman who said she had seen my ad and was hoping I had her Cockapoo. I bit back the snide remark that sprang to mind and told her that the lost animal I had was a dog, not a bird, whereupon she explained, rather indignantly, that Cockapoo is a breed of dog.

After she hung up, I looked in the *Oxford English Dictionary* and there is no entry where "Cockapoo" would be—between "cockamaroo" (a variety of bagatelle) and "cockatiel" (an Australian parrot).

I think the woman made up the word "Cockapoo", and that she herself is best described by the entry immediately prior to cockamaroo; namely, cockamamie.

Susannah said she wasn't asking what had I done about feeding the dog, she was asking what I had done about getting rid of him. "Have you called the shelter yet like you said you were going to?"

"Umm, not exactly."

"What do you mean, not exactly? Either you called them or you didn't."

"I looked up the number."

"And that was as much as you could accomplish today? You're putting off the actual dialing until tomorrow?"

"There's no need to be sarcastic."

"Admit it, Hubie, you're stuck with him."

"I am not stuck with him. I don't want a dog. I don't need the commitment. I want to remain fancy-free." I had been waiting for an opportunity to use that phrase.

In order to avoid discussing the dog, I told Susannah I had looked up "fancy-free" and discovered it was first used by Shakespeare, no less, in a line from *A Midsummer Night's Dream*.

"I wrote this down," I told her and read the passage where Oberon says:

Cupid all arm'd: a certain aim he took
At a fair vestal throned by the west,
And loosed his love-shaft smartly from his bow,
As it should pierce a hundred thousand hearts;
But I might see young Cupid's fiery shaft
Quench'd in the chaste beams of the watery moon,
And the imperial votaress passed on,
In maiden meditation, fancy-free.

"I always love the sound of Shakespeare," she said, "but I never know what it means. To start with, what's a votaress?"

"A female voter?"

She ignored that. "Who was Oberon in the play?"

"I have no idea. I just found the passage in the dictionary. I didn't read the play."

"I've always liked that name. When I was a little girl, I asked my mother if I could change my name to Oberon."

"You read Shakespeare as a little girl?"

"No, silly. I loved Merle Oberon."

"She died years before you were born."

"I know, but her movies were on late night television—*The Scarlet Pimpernel, Dark Angel, Wuthering Heights, A Song to Remember, Désirée*. She was so glamorous. And exotic, too. I read an article about her in one of those movie magazines—*Motion Picture, Modern Screen, Screen Romances*—my mom had boxes of them in the attic."

"So that's why you like old movies so much."

"Yeah, and you like them because you saw them when they were new releases."

I ignored that.

"She always claimed to be Australian," Susannah said.

"Your mother claimed to be Australian?"

"No, Hubert, Merle Oberon did. In fact, her mother was Sinhalese and her father was some philandering British soldier. She grew up in India. But she always tried to hide her true ethnicity. Her dark-skinned mother lived with her, but she pretended to be the maid."

"That's awful!"

"Yeah, and it gets worse. After her mother died, Oberon commissioned someone to do a painting of her."

"There are artists who paint dead people?"

"Don't be ridiculous. He worked from a photograph. He painted her with light skin at Oberon's instruction."

"Oberon is one of the moons of Uranus," I said. It just sort of popped out.

She gave me a funny look. "Oh, right. You and your telescope. What's it look like?"

"It's a long metal tube with—"

"I know what a telescope looks like. What does Oberon the moon look like?"

"Grey, lifeless and pockmarked. Sort of like the dead guy at the morgue."

"Why are we talking about this?"

"Because I was curious about the phrase "fancy-free" and looked it up. It came from a passage in Shakespeare—"

"And you don't want to talk about the dog because you won't admit you're stuck with him."

"I am not stuck with him."

"Of course you are. Let's give him a name."

"He already has a name."

"What is it?"

"He refuses to tell me, but he must have one. His owner must have named him."

"He doesn't have an owner. He doesn't have a collar and no one is looking for him because you've had him in the paper for a week and no one has answered your ad."

"Only six days," I corrected.

"So it's your job to name him."

I threw up my hands in resignation. "Okay, Fearless."

"Fearless?"

"What's wrong with Fearless?"

"Have you looked at him? He should be named after one of the Muppets. Maybe Ernie."

We went around and around about a name and finally agreed on Geronimo. I liked it because that's what parachuters yell as they jump out of the plane, and he had come down into my patio from out of the sky. She liked it because she said the dog looked like that sad picture of Geronimo after he was captured and looked subdued.

I don't know why we both had to agree on a name. After all, he's my dog.

18

"Cupid all arm'd: A certain aim he took, and loosed his love-shaft smartly from his bow, as it should pierce a hundred thousand hearts."

Old Will could certainly turn a phrase. That's exactly how I felt when she walked into my shop. Cupid's dart staggered me.

Then she smiled at me and the room began to spin.

"Come in," I stammered.

She was the sexiest woman I'd ever seen. She was even sexier than the women in the *Sports Illustrated* Swimsuit Edition.

Of course, I'm not interested in sports, so I don't read *Sports Illustrated* and don't know what the women in the Swimsuit Edition look like.

Maybe I've seen a copy on the magazine rack at the grocery store.

I might have even peeked inside out of idle curiosity. I don't remember.

But if I did, I'm sure nothing I saw was anywhere nearly as tantalizing as what was standing in my store smiling at me.

And the weirdest part is she wasn't a classic beauty.

Let's start with her face, a good place to start, although frankly there were no bad places to start. Her face was crooked, her chin not precisely lined up under her nose. Not so out of line that you would call it a defect, but just enough that you noticed it. And her nose bent just slightly to the right, not more than probably a millimeter or two.

Yet it was a face you couldn't stop staring at. Which I was doing, and I thought at any moment she would frown or say something to me about it.

But she didn't. Maybe she was used to it.

She was tall and thin. She had high cheekbones and a great jaw. Who knew a jaw could be sexy?

Her skin had the color of cinnamon and the luster of polished mahogany. Her hair was long and straight. Her eyes were big and dark, the long lashes natural. Her mouth was wide and her lips supple. But what really made her beautiful was the way she moved, unrestrained, comfortable in her skin.

"I love this shop," she said.

"It's yours," I said like an idiot.

I regretted my quip immediately, afraid she would think me a weirdo or pervert, but she laughed and said, "Great. I've always wanted to own a pottery shop."

"Really?"

"Well, no. I saw your wonderful logo and I looked through the window and saw the pots and nothing else. I think that's what I like best, the minimalism."

All these years I've resisted every attempt on the part of wholesalers, jobbers, friends and the Old Town Merchants Association to fill my shop up with other goods—post cards, leather goods, jewelry, key rings, candies. I suppose I could have increased my revenue marginally, but I don't want to be a department store or an upscale convenience store.

So I stuck to my pots-only philosophy, and now it was paying off. It brought *her* into my shop.

She asked me to tell her about the pots, so I came out from behind the counter and did so. It must have taken close to an hour, but she never seemed bored or anxious to leave. Her exotic accent punctuated her many questions.

As we moved from pot to pot, she stood close to me. She would touch my arm occasionally when she wanted to ask me something, and her hair brushed over me several times. None of this seemed flirtatious or even contrived. She was simply at ease, a natural, open, and happy person learning something new.

She smelled of citrus and spices, and the scent lingered after she had gone. I wanted to ask her about herself but couldn't bring myself to do so.

I stared at her as she walked towards the door in long graceful strides, her hair eddying behind her.

Then she turned at the door and said, "What's your name?"

"Hubert."

She smiled. "I'm Izuanita," she said and walked away.

19

Izuanita. An exotic name for an exotic woman, tropical and Aztecan.

I was frozen in place. Perhaps I hoped she'd come back.

"Are you okay?"

Susannah had materialized in my doorway.

"Hi. The most amazing woman was just in here."

"Are you expecting her back? Is that why you were staring at the door?"

"No. Yes. I don't know."

"It's five thirty. I was getting worried about you. When I saw you just standing there, I thought when you finally opened your mouth you'd have slurred speech and your left arm wouldn't move."

"As it should pierce a hundred thousand hearts." I said.

"Huh?"

"I'll explain it to you over a margarita."

Once we were seated in Dos Hermanas, I told her all about Izuanita.

"Wow! You are smitten."

She was right. I've had my share of romances, I suppose, though most of them have been short-lived. And although I honestly believe all women are beautiful, each in her own way, I have to admit that a few of the women I've known have been more beautiful than most.

But smitten? Not like this.

I described her in detail to Susannah who took in every word. If there's one thing she likes better than murder mysteries, it's romances. Not the books, the real thing.

"How old is she?"

"I have no idea."

"Take a guess."

"Somewhere between eighteen and forty five."

She laughed. "Did you introduce her to Geronimo?"

"No."

"You should. Most women are suckers for dogs."

"How do they feel about anteaters?"

"Now that's the old Hubie we all know and love. I was worried that your goddess had knocked your personality out of whack."

"Did I tell you I offered to give her my shop?"

"Geez, I wish I had that effect on men. You're never late for drinks. Then I find you in a trance. I thought you'd had a stroke."

"No. Just a heart attack."

"Well, tell your heart not to worry. You'll see her again."

"You really think so?"

"Take it from me. She didn't give you her name just because she likes saying it."

We moved from Izuanita the Goddess to Chris the handsome Italian with the fractured English.

"And was he right," I asked, "that La Hacienda is a 'luminary for its fabrication of local repasts?'"

She shook her head. "His strange English doesn't seem to matter to women. The waitress fawned over him all night."

"So we know the service was excellent—"

"A little too excellent."

"How was the food?"

"It wouldn't be professional of me to say anything about the food since I work at their competitor, La Placita."

"In other words, you didn't even notice."

"Okay, so I didn't notice. How could I? I was too busy trying to make conversation. He asked me at one point why I was a fractional devotee of art history. I mean, how do you answer a question like that?"

"Did you ever figure out what he meant by that?"

"I did. And you would have been proud of my ingenuity. What I did was start answering all his questions with questions, and eventually I got enough info to know how to respond. But I made sure the questions were actually compliments because I didn't want him to think I was criticizing his English."

"For example?"

"When he asked why I was a fractional devotee of art history, I told him I was impressed that he noticed. Then I asked what had led him to suspect that I might be. His answer mentioned my work as a waitress, and then I asked about that, and so on, and finally I realized he was asking me why I'm a part-time student."

"That was ingenious, but you can't go on like that. You either have to help him or get someone else to."

"I don't want to be the one to correct Chris' English. Teacher/ student is not compatible with girlfriend/boyfriend. Maybe I could arrange for someone else to take on the task without Chris knowing I had anything to do with it."

She smiled at me across the top of her saltless margarita glass.

"Oh, no. Not me. I'd do almost anything for you Susannah, but not that. No, definitely not."

"Come on, Hubie. The guy hasn't made a pass at me. He hasn't even held my hand. And no wonder. I'm too busy trying to understand him to flirt with him."

The conversation continued for a while and the final upshot of it was that I agreed to meet Chris on Thursday afternoon.

I sang under my breath as I walked across the Plaza on my way home. The song was *Black Magic* and the words were:

Izuanita has me in her spell,
That Aztec magic that she weaves so well
Those icy fingers up and down my spine,
The longing feeling when her eyes meet mine.

So I modified the lyrics slightly. I also didn't sound exactly like Frank Sinatra, but I wasn't doing a public performance, so who cares? There was a spring in my step because Susannah convinced me that I would see Izuanita again.

But what I saw instead was a white van coming down my street and then turning towards Central and disappearing out of sight. The words "United Plumbing" were in big black letters.

20

Someone in old town had their sink overflow while doing the dinner dishes, and the plumber they called to unclog their drains just happened to be the same one I'd seen three times on Titanium Trail where they were doing . . . what?

Installing a new water heater?

Maybe.

Or maybe watching me watch Cantú's condo?

But why?

I puzzled about it long into the night and all I got out of it was bags under my eyes the next day.

I called Martin at the tribal store the next morning and left him a message. When he called an hour later, I asked how much he wanted for his Uncle's pot. He told me twenty-five hundred, and I told him I had the money to buy it because I'd finally made a sale, a small plate from Santo Domingo that brought three thousand dollars.

He showed up around four that afternoon. There were three people in the store—a man and wife arguing about where to eat and their teenage daughter tuning them out in favor of something she was listening to via earphones.

Martin looked at the couple and said, "I come here trade pot for wampum."

The arguing couple forgot their dispute. The husband grabbed his wife's hand and led her out. The teenage daughter remained. She took off the headphone and said, "Are you a real Native American?"

He said he was and she said, "This is so cool."

"Would you like to buy the pot?" Martin asked her.

"My dumb parents never give me any money."

"Tiffany! Get out here immediately," her mother called from out on the sidewalk.

"Can I have your autograph," Tiffany asked Martin.

"Sure," he said. "Where you want me to sign?"

She pulled her right sleeve up and handed Martin a black marker pen. "Right here," she said, indicating a place on her shoulder. "Try to make it as even and level as you can. I'm going to have a tattoo artist trace over it before I wash it off, so what you write will be permanent."

Martin hesitated for a moment, then shrugged and signed her shoulder while the parents looked on from outside in horror.

Tiffany sidled up to one of my display cases and looked at her shoulder's reflection in the glass. "This will be the coolest tattoo in history. Thanks, Mister Bull," she said and ran out overjoyed.

"Mr. Bull?" I said after she left.

"I signed it Sitting Bull," he said.

I paid Martin the twenty-five hundred and placed the pot in one of the display cases with "five thousand dollars" written on the tented card in front of it. Like all the best restaurants, I write the prices out in words rather than numbers.

It was almost five, so Martin and I walked over to Dos Hermanas to meet Susannah who was happy to see him.

After Susannah and I had our margaritas and Martin his Tecate, he turned to me and asked, "You finish that book I gave you?"

"You gave it to me? I thought you just loaned it to me."

"He's on page five," said Susannah.

"Good thing I gave it to you. The rate you reading it, I'll never see it again."

"I'm a potter, not a physicist."

"It's not written for physicists. It's written for what you white people call the educated layman."

"I'm white," Susannah said, "and I've never called anybody that."

That brought a chuckle from Martin.

"What did you get from the first five pages?" Martin asked me.

"If you throw an electron, you never know which way it might go."

"You can't throw electrons," he replied.

"That's what I told him," said Susannah.

"What about those electron guns?" I said. "They throw electrons."

Martin nodded. "Suppose you throw a baseball at a piece of plywood. The ball makes a little dent in the wood. If you could duplicate that throw exactly with a second throw, you'd expect the ball to hit right in that first dent."

"You haven't seen him throw a ball," Susannah interjected. "He couldn't hit the plywood, much less the dent."

"Okay," said Martin, "I'll let you throw it."

"Thanks," she said.

"So you throw two baseballs exactly the same way, and they hit the same spot. Now imagine that instead of baseballs, we throw electrons."

"Must be hard to get a two-seam grip on those puppies," said Susannah. She and Martin had a fine laugh, and I took a sip of my margarita. I figured her remark was some sort of inside joke, but I wasn't about to ask what it meant.

Martin continued, "Even if the electron gun is aimed exactly at the same place, the "dents" are not the same. Each electron hits in a different place."

Susannah shrugged. "So?"

"Doesn't strike you as odd that two electrons start off in the same place, leave the gun at the same speed pointed in the same directions and end up at different locations?"

"Not really. The baseballs travel the same path because they're big. But the electrons are so small they get pushed around by solar winds or magnetic forces or light waves or something, so they get bumped off course."

Martin looked at me. "I think you should give her the book."

"I don't want it," she said before I could respond. Then she waved for Angie. While we were waiting for refills, she said, "Look at us. One part-time night student, one guy who got expelled and one who dropped out at age thirteen, all having a grand time at the bar discussing subatomic particles. We need to get lives, guys."

"This is life," I said. "Part of life is about figuring things out."

"Things that matter, Hubie. I guess people building nuclear reactors have to worry about electrons, but the rest of us have more important things to figure out."

"I didn't believe all triangles have interior angles equal to 180 degrees when Mr. Matthews told me that in the fourth grade. I figured there are so many different triangles—long skinny ones, squashed flat ones, etc.—that their interior angles couldn't always be the same. But when he showed me the proof, it suddenly made sense to me."

"Your fourth grade class did geometry proofs?" asked Martin.

"Not the whole class. Mr. Matthews gave extra sessions after school for kids who were interested in math, donating his own time. Sometimes he smelled of what I later came to realize was rye whisky, but in those days I just thought he was sleepy and had bad breath. But on the days when he was alert, it was like magic to me, the idea that you could prove something with absolute certainty."

"I had teachers like that," said Martin, "I would've stayed in school."

"I wouldn't have given up my after-school time," said Susannah. "Proofs may be certain, but nothing in real life is, and that's what makes it interesting."

21

Geronimo was waiting for me. I could hear him scratching at the patio door.

I popped the cork on a Gruet *Blanc de Noir* and opened a box of dog biscuits. I took a sniff and decided the biscuits didn't go with champagne, so I grabbed a box of piñon brittle I'd bought from a shop a few doors to the east, the same one where I buy my piñon aftershave.

It was cool out in the patio. Geronimo sniffed the dog biscuits and came to the same conclusion I had. However, he was having them with water, not champagne, so I told him he'd have to make the best of it.

I sipped the Gruet and looked up at the stars. I opened the piñon brittle. Geronimo looked up at me hopefully.

"Only after you finish your biscuit," I told him, and damned if he didn't wolf down the biscuit. He's smarter than he looks.

I gave him a large piece of brittle. When he crunched it, it flew in all directions. I guess that's why they call it brittle. It didn't faze him, though. He chewed the part he had bitten off and then went around picking up all the pieces with his sticky tongue. I swear he's part anteater.

When I was a kid, I used to sneak out of the house after my parents were asleep. I lay in the grass and looked up at the stars. There wasn't as much light pollution back then, and you could see all the major constellations.

The skies are not as clear now, but because there's no moisture in the air and we're a mile high, the atmosphere is still easier to see through than most urban locations, and the wall around my patio has a bit of the "well effect." So I sat there looking up at the twinkling stars and wondering if they were really composed of zillions of subatomic particles zooming around in random directions.

The champagne was cold and crisp and the piñon brittle hard and sweet, so I had a little more of each.

And woke up sometime in the middle of the night asleep in my lawn chair. Geronimo had taken advantage of my slumber to finish off the piñon brittle.

"You are grounded," I told him as I staggered inside. I dreamed of Izuanita, but it would be less than gallant for me to share the details of that dream. I can say that at one point she was standing close to me with her long arms on my shoulders, her scent around me like a cloud from Xochimilco.

There was a rhythmic beating. Perhaps native drums. Perhaps my heart pounding at her nearness.

Perhaps someone at the door. I covered my head with one of my pillows. Go away, I said telepathically to the early-bird customer. I don't care if I miss a sale, just go away.

But he kept pounding.

I rolled out of bed, donned my robe and made it to the front door where I saw Whit Fletcher.

"You got a warrant," I said after opening the door.

"What kind of question is that?" he asked, feigning hurt. "I drop by to see an old friend and you want to know if I got a warrant." He shook his head in disappointment at my cynicism.

"Okay," I said, "no warrant. How about coffee?"

"Now that's more like it. I could use a good cupa Joe. How about you put the pot on?"

"I meant did you *bring* coffee," I muttered to myself as he followed me back to my kitchen. I lit the fire under the coffee pot I had primed the night before and excused myself for my morning ablutions.

When I returned, Whit had made himself comfortable in my willow chaise, so I took one of the less comfortable kitchen chairs after pouring us both a cup of Café Bustelo, two bucks a pound and better than the stuff that sells for five times as much. It's roasted to Latin American tastes and holds up well to lots of cream and sugar.

"I been thinking about what you said before we went to the morgue," he said.

"I said a lot of things before we went to the morgue, but none of them did any good because you made me go anyway."

"I didn't make you go. You was just doing your duty as a citizen."

"Right."

"What I'm talking about is when you asked me why we thought you might be able to ID the guy."

"You said it was police business and nothing I needed to know."

He pushed a mop of silver hair off his forehead. "That's still true officially. Let's agree right now that's what you'll say if anyone asks you about it."

I nodded.

"Fact is, the dead guy was a pot collector. So naturally, we figured you'd know him."

I felt a freshet of relief. Premature as it turned out.

"He collected those real old pots. You know those whatyamacallits—the ones you dig up illegally."

"Anasazi," I said.

He smiled at me. "If you didn't know him, how'd you know he collected Anasazi?"

"You just said so."

"I said whatyamacallits."

"Nice try," I said. "You also said the kind I dig up, and almost all of those are Anasazi."

"That's okay, Hubert. I still think you know him, but I won't press it." He took a sip of his coffee. "How much one of those pots worth these days?"

So that's why he'd come by, the scent of money. "Depends on its condition," I said. "One in good shape can bring fifty thousand."

He whistled softly in admiration of a fifty thousand dollar pot. "That guy you saw at the morgue—the one you say you didn't know—he had twenty-five old pots. I don't know if they was Anasazi or not. You'd be the one to know that. And I don't know if they was in good shape. Most of 'em had nicks and cracks and some had big pieces missin', but maybe that's good shape considering how old they are. I guess you'd be the one to know about that, too. But I know there was twenty-five of 'em because I counted them myself. So even if they weren't all good enough to bring fifty thousand, that collection is worth at least half a million."

I sipped my coffee and said nothing.

"The way I figure it, those pots don't have anything to do with him being poisoned—"

"Poisoned?"

"What'd you think? He died of natural causes?"

"I guess I just assumed he'd been shot or knifed or something."

"You see any holes in him?"

"He was covered with a sheet, remember?"

"I guess you did have your eyes open after all. Anyway, if he'd been killed for the pots, they'd be gone. So if they weren't the motive, then they ain't evidence. I don't know who has claim to them, but I figure nobody but the original collector knows exactly how many pots was in the collection, and if a few of the better ones were to go missing, what's the harm? What I'm sayin' is I may be able to lay my hands on a few of these pots and no one's gonna squeal about it."

I was still sipping coffee.

"But I'd need an expert to tell me the best ones to select. And I'd need someone to sell them. On the sly, so to speak. And you and me have done a few deals in the past that always worked out pretty good, so I was thinking . . ."

I didn't hear what he was thinking because the coffee was gradually lifting the fog, and I realized that what he said implied he had seen the collection.

When he stopped talking, I asked him when the guy had been poisoned.

"We found him on Sunday, but he hadn't been doing any praying. Coroner said he'd been dead ten to twelve hours, so he must have died late Saturday night or early Sunday morning."

The house had been empty on Thursday, three days *before* the police discovered the dead guy. My head started spinning. How had Whit seen the pots?

22

"I told you that wasn't the house."

"You never said that," I countered.

"Well, maybe not in so many words, but I always thought you were too confident."

"I'm still confident. That was the house."

"Then how come the pots were gone on Thursday and back on Sunday when Whit got there?"

I was ready for that one. "Because they took the pots before Thursday. Then, when the guy died, they figured they better put them back. After the heat's off, they'll take them again."

She gave me a look of total incredulity. "You have got to be kidding me. Why would they put the pots back after they killed the guy?"

It was time to explain my brilliant theory. "They didn't kill him. They took the pots sometime after my appraisal and before I went back in on Thursday. They were home free. Then somebody murdered the guy on Saturday night or Sunday morning, so they brought the pots back because if they got caught with the pots, the police might also tag them with the murder, thinking they had killed him to get the pots."

Susannah rolled her eyes skyward then took a drink from her margarita. Then she took a long slow deep breath. "Hubert," she said, "this is bizarre even by your standards. First, who are the 'they' who took the pots? Second, who are the 'they' that killed the guy? And third, why would the first 'theys'—the ones who took the pots—feel like they had to put them back after the second 'theys' killed the guy?"

Somehow it sounded less convincing the way she said it. But I wasn't ready to admit defeat. I may be only 5' 6" and 140 pounds, but I'm still a man, and we don't easily admit to being mistaken.

"I don't know who the 'they' were who took the pots, but I know the pots were gone, so there has to be a 'they' who took them. Then a second 'they'—or a him or a her—killed the guy. It can't be the first 'they' or him or her, because if you already have the pots, why go back and kill the guy?"

She stared at me for a while. Finally she said, "Here's a better theory. The pots didn't belong to Cantú. They never did. They were never in that house you broke in to. They were in another house and they're still there."

"But the house I broke in to was the house where I did the appraisal." Except I think I may have pronounced it "appwaisal." I was on my fourth margarita, still trying to deal with the shock of what Whit had told me.

"Face it. It was not the house."

"But it was exactly like it."

"All the houses in *Casitas del Bosque* are exactly like it. They're cookie-cutter houses. That's why they all have the back window in the same place."

"And the same cream-colored shade?"

"Yep."

"And the same fireplace?"

She nodded.

"And the same beige carpet?"

"The developer probably got a great deal on a bulk purchase."

"Even the shelves?"

"What else would you put on the sides of a fireplace?"

I took another drink from my margarita. Probably a mistake. I was already feeling queasy. "So the pots are in another house in *Casitas del Bosque*?"

She leaned back in her chair and gave a slight nod. The nod may have been slight, but the triumph behind it was palpable.

"That seems way too coincidental. I mean, what are the odds that Cantú, who asked me to copy three of the pots, lived in the same condominimum edition as the guy who actually owned them and got killed?"

"I think you mean 'condominium addition.'"

"That's what I said."

"No, you said 'condominimum edition,' like it was an issue of a magazine dealing with very small condoms."

I was totally confused.

"Actually," she continued, "it's not coincidental at all. If the collector was a recluse and wanted someone to take the pots to be copied, he would probably choose a neighbor. What would be surprising would be if Cantú *didn't* live near the collector. It's just like I said from the beginning. Cantú was just the errand boy. You wasted all that time watching his house, and you even stole his car."

"But it still seems suspiciously coincidental that Cantú picks this time to move. How do you explain that?"

"Easy. The collector gave Cantú some money for helping with the sale of the pots and Cantú decided to move to a better neighborhood."

"And leave his car?"

"That part is odd. Wait a minute! Maybe Cantú is the murderer!"

Here we go again, I thought to myself.

"It makes sense," she said. "He kills the collector for the pots and then leaves town. He can't make his getaway in his own car, so he buys a new one, or borrows one, or rents one, or steals one . . . no, he wouldn't steal one . . . but he gets another car and leaves."

"So he doesn't want to take his car because he's on the lam and wants to get out of town fast."

"Exactly," she said.

"But he takes the time to pack up all his belongings?"

"Maybe he was really attached to them."

"Face it. Neither one of us has a clue what's going on."

"I guess you're right."

Susannah walked me home. Out the front door of Dos Hermanas. Across the street and up a block to the Plaza. Diagonally across the Plaza to my street then a block down on the left to the entrance to my shop. Just past the United Plumbing van on the right.

When I got inside, I brushed my teeth and splashed some cold water on my face. It sobered me up enough to tell Susannah about the United Plumbing van.

Being a Woman of Action, she handed me the phone book and ordered me to look up United Plumbing.

Turns out there are about two hundred plumbing firms in Albuquerque. There are small one-person operations, franchises like Roto-Rooter, big mechanical contractors, air-conditioning experts, and firms that specialize in one thing like backyard spas.

The variety amazed me. You can get a plumber in this town to do just about anything. Some are even available twenty-four hours a day. Some are radio-dispatched. All of them are licensed and most are bonded.

Well, you wouldn't put "not bonded" in a yellow page ad, would you?

The names of the companies include unimaginative ones like A-1 Plumbing and companies named after their owners like Pacheco's Plumbing. Then there were some with cutesy names like All Knight Plumbing, Drain Busters, Flo Right, H2O Services, Pipes R Us (they didn't have the "R" turned backwards), and my personal favorite, Plumbology.

I am not making this up.

Finally, there were some names you would find only in New Mexico: like Zia, Coyote, Desert Sky, Cactus, and my favorite as an anthropologist—Petroglyph Plumbing.

There's one kind of plumber Albuquerque doesn't have—one named United.

23

When I woke up on Thursday morning, a family of desert badgers were having a burrowing contest in my cranium.

Susannah must have readied my coffee—I'm pretty certain I didn't—so I hit the brew button, took off my undies and turned the shower on full blast. After the hot water had warmed the tile floor in the shower, I sat down and let the water cascade over me for maybe twenty minutes.

I didn't even bother to towel off. I just wrapped myself in my robe, filled a mug with hot black coffee, and staggered out to my patio. My fuzzy-brained plan had been to sit in the warm morning sun and sip coffee until the headache went away.

What I had forgotten was that there was another headache in the patio by the name of Geronimo. It was bad enough that he tried to lick me to death, but did you ever hear of a dog that drank hot coffee?

I had to get a fresh cup and then I had to stand up to keep it out of his reach. I was in the midst of cursing him for interfering with my hangover recovery when I realized it had gone away.

The hangover, not the dog.

So I stood there feeling the warm morning sun as it peeked over the east side of my patio wall.

And realized Susannah was right. Cantú's house was not where I had appraised the pots. When she and I had gone there, me blindfolded in her Crown Vic, I had been convinced it was the right house. It was Cantú's address as listed in the phone book. The location seemed right, about the same amount of time and number of turns as my first blindfolded ride. The size of the house seemed right. The back window was in the right place. The door was the right distance from the curb. I was positive it was the place. But you may remember me mentioning a nagging feeling in the back of my mind that some small detail was wrong. Now I knew what that detail was.

I felt like an idiot for not thinking of it sooner, but I felt great that I knew it now because for the first time since my twenty-five hundred dollars disappeared, I could see how I might be able to get it back. And maybe a lot more.

I shaved, brushed, flossed, and gave myself a few spritzes of piñon cologne. The shop that sells it also offers cactus flower, yucca, and midnight cereus.

Ah yes, midnight cereus. A flower of legend. It's a cactus, and for 364 days a year it does its imitation of a dead stick. But on one night each year, it blooms. And what a bloom it is—full, white and spiky. Resembling a water lily, it releases its intoxicating scent then closes forever with the rising sun.

Because I often dig for pots at night, I've seen the bloom on several occasions. It is spectacular. But like other plants, it also has a root, not nearly as interesting to look at but much tastier than the flower. Some Native Americans eat the root, and some wacko ecologists want to make eating it illegal because they claim the plant is endangered. I don't know if the plant is endangered or not, but if it is, it's not because it is eaten. It's because it's difficult for a plant to propagate when its flower has only a few hours a year to be pollinated and this occurs when most insects are asleep.

My hunch is that the cologne called midnight cereus is not made from the actual flower. But piñon is common enough and smells clean and sweet, so I adopted it many years ago as my signature scent.

I looked good, smelled good, and felt good.

I went outside and leaned against my new Cadillac. Well, not mine exactly. But Susannah had rigged up a switch so that I could start it and drive it whenever I wanted to.

In addition to my piñon aftershave, there was another scent in the air, tropical and citrusy. I turned upwind and she was there, striding towards me with that easy, self-assured gait, like a fashion model on a runway except without the insouciance. Instead of the aloof expression of models, a laughing smile playing across her sensual lips, and her long hair frolicked in the morning breeze.

Her stride was confident and natural. A song played in my head.

Tall and tan and young and lovely
The girl from Ipanema goes walking
And when she passes
Each one she passes goes aaah
When she walks it's like a samba
That sways so sweet and swings so gently
That when she passes
Each one she passes goes aaah

Except she wasn't from Ipanema. She was from the city of Tenoch-titlan on the island in Lake Texcoco. Long limbed and lean. Sinewy and sexy. Also known as Izuanita.

"Hi, Hubert."

Be calm, I told myself. Be cool.

"Hi," I answered.

So far, so good.

"Is this your car?"

"No. I'm just keeping it for somebody."

She put one of those long lean hands lightly on my forearm, "Can we go for a ride in it?"

"Just what I was thinking," I said. At least I didn't offer to give her the car. But I did remember what Susannah told me about girls and dogs, so I said, "Would you mind if my dog came along? He loves to go for rides."

"I love dogs."

I went to the patio and put Geronimo's new lead on his new collar. On the way back to the front, I said to him, "Don't blow this if you know what's good for you."

He stood up when he saw her, placing his front paws on her chest—sly dog—and she hugged him and then started rubbing his ears. When she stopped and he calmed down a little, I pulled him back.

When all four paws were back on the ground, she said, "Maybe you should take that bandana off. It makes his neck seem sort of long."

After I had removed the bandana, she stared at Geronimo for a moment.

"Now it seems even longer." She looked at me and smiled. "Maybe you should put it back."

I did and opened the door for Izuanita. Geronimo weaseled in before she did—no manners at all—and went straight to the driver's seat. I held the door for Izuanita and then went around to the driver's side. I pushed Geronimo into the back seat and slid behind the wheel, wondering how I would explain the jerry-rigged switch. But she didn't ask about it.

Instead she asked, "Can we put the top down?"

Sure, I thought to myself. If I can figure out how to do it.

"Like I said," I explained, "I'm just keeping it for someone else. I'm not sure I know how to—"

Whereupon she reached up to the top of the windshield, threw back a couple of lever looking devices and then leaned across me and threw a switch that was on the left side of the dashboard next to the light switch.

I briefly reflected on the fact that both Susannah and Izuanita knew more about cars than I did, but my primary thought arose from the "leaning across me" part of what happened. She was so at ease that I thought she truly did not recognize how sexy she was.

The good news was that the effort to reach a switch on the far left of the dashboard resulted in her being very close to me, and she stayed there even though her assistance in lowering the top was no longer needed.

Geronimo took advantage of the situation to jump into the front seat and ride shotgun. I didn't care. As long as he didn't try to take the middle between Izuanita and me, he could sit wherever he pleased.

"How about some music?" she asked as we turned onto Central.

"I don't know if the radio works," I admitted.

"Let's play a tape," she said. Then she opened the glove compartment and rummaged through some old cassettes until she found one she liked. It must have been one of those collections they sell on television because it had a bit of everything on it.

The ones I recognized were *You've Made Me So Very Happy* by Blood Sweat & Tears, *Down On The Corner* by Creedence Clearwater Revival, *Put A Little Love In Your Heart* by Jackie DeShannon, *Sweet Caroline* by Neil Diamond, *Lay Lady Lay* by Bob Dylan, *Aquarius* by The Fifth Dimension, and *Someday We'll Be Together* by The Supremes. None of them my kind of music—I'm more into Ella Fitzgerald than Diana Ross—but all of them tunes I'd heard because they are still on the play lists of some radio stations in Albuquerque.

The only radio I listen to these days comes to me from a satellite, but you can't escape other people's radios when you walk or ride anywhere these days, so you hear them whether you like it or not. It's usually not, but I have to admit it was fun listening to these golden oldies.

Of course doing so while driving in a 1969 Cadillac convertible with a beautiful woman by my side probably added to the festive youthful feeling that washed over me.

If you're paying attention, you noticed that I remembered seven of the songs on the tape Izuanita popped into the cassette slot of the radio. There were several others I didn't recognize, so if you do the math, you might think we went a long ways. In fact, we took a short drive over to the Hurricane Drive-In on Lomas, but we let the music play while we ate.

The Hurricane was Izuanita's suggestion. Except for chips and salsa, I hadn't eaten anything since lunch the previous day, so The Hurricane sounded just right. The place has a red and white metal sign with incandescent light bulbs so you know it must have been erected in the fifties. I don't think anyone has touched it since. If you looked only at the sign, you'd assume the place was out of business, but if you look at the drive-in spaces next to the menus and the speakers, there are always cars.

Albuquerqueans ignore the beat up sign and crowded conditions because sometimes we hanker for a simpler time when cholesterol and carbohydrates were words know only to chemists. The most popular dish is called the Disaster Burritos. It begins as a flour tortilla rolled up and stuffed with beef and beans. Then it's covered with curly French fries smothered in a combination of cheddar and Monterrey jack cheeses. The behemoth is then covered with lettuce and tomatoes in a futile attempt to introduce a salad-healthy touch to this calorie bomb. It's so big most people order the one-quarter size. It's disgusting when you think about it. And irresistible.

When I told her I was starving, Izuanita bet me she could eat as much as I could, so we ordered a whole one and split it fifty-fifty.

When the last of the Disaster Burrito had disappeared, she said, "I told you I could finish my half."

"You cheated. You gave some to Geronimo."

"How could I resist those sad eyes?"

"He's a shameless beggar. You shouldn't encourage him. Where to now?"

"Home, James,"

"Your home or mine?"

"Isn't that line supposed to be 'Your *place* or mine?'"

She laughed and I laughed. Then she made a trip to the ladies room and returned with fresh lipstick and the shiniest red nails ever seen.

"Good thing the top's down. I can dry my nails."

She hadn't answered my question about which home she was to be taken to, and since I didn't know where hers was, I drove back to mine. She turned the volume up and sat close to me. She put her arm around my back, and it was so long that her hand extended beyond the door. I didn't know whether the object was to dry the nail polish or have her arm around me, although I suspected it was the former.

Her right arm was extended in the opposite direction past Geronimo whose long neck was craned out to take in as much air as possible, and I suppose his coat was also being whipped by the wind, but thankfully none of it was lashing my face.

I had a new car, a new dog and a new girlfriend. The world was a perfect place.

Of course the dog was a misshapen mutt, the car was—let's be honest here—was stolen, and Izuanita being my girlfriend was more wish than fact.

When I pulled up in front of my shop, Geronimo jumped into the back seat and hunkered down as low as he could against the floor, obviously hoping the ride was not over and his time in the Caddy not at an end.

Izuanita, unfortunately, did not share his hesitancy to abandon ship. When I opened the door, she stepped out and said, "Why did you name him Geronimo?"

"Because Geronimo was a fearless warrior."

She laughed and hugged me with those long arms. "I love your sense of humor," she said.

Then she thanked me for the ride and the food and walked away. I guess I could have asked her to stay or yelled for her to come back.

But I didn't. I just stood there watching her disappear around the corner. There was something about her self-assurance that brooked no resistance when she decided to leave. I got the feeling she would come and go as she pleased, and I didn't mind. In fact, I liked it. It was who she was. If a female Quetzalcoatl deigns to fly into your life, you don't try to cage her.

Just before she reached the corner, a handsome young fellow came around it in my direction and nodded to Izuanita as they passed.

Then he walked up to me and said, "I assert with surety that you are Mr. Hubert Schuze."

You know who it was.

"You must be Chris," I replied.

"This makes a large indention in me. How did this knowledge coalesce?"

I smiled at him as I remembered how Susannah had managed to translate by asking questions. "I think maybe the word you want is 'impression' rather than 'indention,'" I said.

After Susannah cajoled me into meeting with Chris, I had given some thought to the approach I would take. I decided that since I had no relationship with him to worry about, I would point out his unidiomatic language right from the start and try to correct him. If he responded positively to that, then the problem would eventually be solved. If he was offended, then he could choose not to meet with me again. I didn't know which one I hoped for.

"'Indention' and 'impression' are coextensive are they not?"

"They are not."

"Forgive the refutation, but the dictionary pleads that 'impression' is 'a mark produced on a surface by pressure,' and 'indention' is offered as 'the condition of being indented' or 'a dent.'"

"Perhaps. But an indention is always physical. The only way I could make an indention on you would be to hit you with a hammer."

He smiled at that.

"But an impression," I continued, "can be either physical or mental. So I impressed you by recognizing you. I didn't indent you."

"This is animating. Perhaps please you can convalesce my English?"

It was going to be a long afternoon.

24

"The problem," I told her, "is that he learned English from a dictionary. That and his eidetic memory."

"What's an eidetic memory?"

"A photographic memory."

"Why not just say so? Or did Chris arouse your male competitiveness, and you're trying to prove you know as many weird words as he does?"

"You know I'm not competitive, and anyway, I'd lose that one. He uses words I've never heard. I told you he saw Izuanita on the sidewalk? Well, he described her as a Modigliani woman. I looked it up in my dictionary but couldn't find it."

Susannah started laughing.

"Of course," I said, slapping myself on the forehead, "it's Italian. I should have picked up on that from the sound of it."

"It's Italian alright, but it's not a word. It's a name. He was an artist, Hubie. I can't believe you never heard of him."

"Did he paint anything famous?"

"He painted a lot of women."

"Well that narrows it down. Any famous paintings of women like *Mona Lisa* or *Whistler's Mother?*"

"There's no painting called Whistler's Mother. It's called *Arrangement in Grey and Black.*"

"I'm glad we cleared that up. What about Modigliani?"

"There's no single painting he's known by. You didn't by any chance rip Izuanita's bodice did you, because Modigliani painted a lot of nudes."

"I resisted the temptation."

"There's another thing he's famous for. His women often had distorted faces like the way you described Izuanita to me."

I was shocked. "I did not say her face is *distorted,*" I replied rather more forcefully than I meant to. "It's just not perfectly symmetrical, and that only adds to the exotic—"

"Yeah, I know, she looks like an Aztecan Goddess."

"She looked even better in the Cadillac."

"Where did you take her?"

"The Hurricane."

She plopped her margarita onto the table. "That must have impressed her."

"It was her idea."

"Did she order a Disaster Burrito?"

"She said she could eat as much as I could, so we ordered one and split it fifty-fifty. She ate her half, but I actually won because she gave part of hers to Geronimo, and I ate my half all by myself."

"This from a man who's not competitive. Was I right about the dog?"

"Yeah, she loves him. I'm not sure how she feels about me."

I told her everything about my morning with Izuanita.

Then I told her she was right about Cantú's house.

"I was there in the evening, and even though no lights were on, I was able to examine the pots easily because of the bright sunlight streaming through the window. When you drove me there, we saw what I thought was that window when we went around to the back of the place. But we were driving south and the window was on our left."

"So?"

"So the window faces east. There couldn't have been any bright evening sun coming through it."

"How do you know we were driving south?"

"Because the Sandias were on our left."

"I'll take your word for that."

"And that means you were right," I admitted. "It must be a different house in *Casitas del Bosque*."

"On the opposite side of the street."

"Exactly."

She gave me that mischievous smile. "So all you have to do is break in to every house on the opposite side of the street until you find the one with the pots."

"There's an easier way. I'll just get the address from Whit."

"Which he'll give you because he wants you to steal some of the pots."

"The way he sees it," I corrected her, "is that no one knows how many pots were in that collection, so what difference does it make if we take a few and sell them."

"And how do you see it?"

I shrugged and said, "Depends on whether the dead guy has heirs. If he does, then taking the pots would definitely be stealing."

"And you won't do that."

I shook my head. "But I might take back my copies."

"Why? He paid for them didn't he?"

"It looks that way. I know Cantú was the one who handed me the money, but it appears you were right that he was just the errand boy, so the collector was the one who had them copied. Then the collector sold the originals because he needed money, and he kept the copies so his collection appeared to remain intact."

"That was your original theory."

"And still the best," I boasted. "So here's my issue. What's going to happen to the collection? Suppose he had heirs and they want the cash instead of the pots."

"Who wouldn't choose a million bucks over a bunch of old cracked pots?"

"Me," I said.

"Yeah, but you're sort of a cracked pot yourself."

She said it with a smile and I didn't argue the point. "So they auction off the pots. The person or persons who bought the three originals would likely be interested, and when they see the pots they think they bought are still in the collection—"

"They'll think they've been swindled!"

"Exactly. They won't be able to tell the fakes from the originals, so they'll assume the collector sold them fakes."

"Can't they run lab tests or something?"

"Sure. But before they reach that point there's going to be a lot of confusion, accusation and argument. And guess whose name is going to be dragged in?"

"So what's your plan?"

"If I take the fakes, then the person or persons who own the originals won't have to fight over what they have and whether it's genuine. I won't have to get involved with the police, the probate court, the heirs, the collectors or anyone else. The heirs will have the original pots they inherited and the collectors will have the three pots they bought."

"And you'll have your copies."

"Exactly."

"Which you already got paid for."

"Yeah, and now I can get paid for them again. The guy who bought them still owes me an appraisal fee. The only thing that's changed is the fee just got a lot higher."

She held her glass up and I clinked mine against it.

"What about the Cadillac?" she asked.

"I'll drive it back to 183 Titanium Trail and leave it in the garage."

"Won't Izuanita be disappointed when she finds out you don't own a Cadillac convertible?"

"She already knows that. I told her I was keeping it for someone."

Susannah dredged a large chip through the salsa and popped it into her mouth. After she swallowed, she said, "Tell me more about your English lesson with Chris."

"It wasn't an English lesson, and I hope you didn't tell him it was."

She shook her head.

"You were right about him being handsome. He looks like he could be a model for a really upscale men's clothing catalog."

"I know," she said dreamily, "and he has great manners. You don't see that much these days."

"Except he sort of invades your space."

"That's not bad manners, Hubie. That's just Europe, especially Italy."

"So I've heard. Anyway, he's a good conversationalist except for his odd word choices."

"And you helped with that, right?"

"I tried to. He didn't seem the least bit offended by my constantly correcting him. And he did something I really liked. After I told him the correct usage of a word, he would work that word into the conversation a few minutes later. I think that shows he wants to improve."

"What did you talk about?"

"Etruscan pottery."

"Why am I not surprised?"

"Chris liked the pots in my shop. He said they reminded him of ancient Etruscan pots. He's from Florence. I guess that's in the area where the ancient Etruscans lived. He said their pots are black, red, and sienna shades. They're decorated with geometric patterns. I told him that some work from the pueblos—"

"Hubie?"

"Yes?"

"Can we get another round?"

"Sure."

"And another topic."

"Sure."

25

I drove slowly along Titanium Trail and looked at the houses with even numbers. They looked just like the ones with odd numbers—the same clusters of six, the same wrought iron numbers on the same plank doors, the same fake buttresses that had nothing to buttress and the same ugly stucco, especially the mustard color.

The only difference was that the odd-numbered houses faced east, and that meant their rear windows faced west, and that meant . . . well, I already explained that.

I was in the Bronco because I figured everyone on the street would recognize Cantú's Cadillac, and on top of that the Cadillac was no longer at my disposal because I had driven it nine miles away and parked it in a location where no state trooper or Albuquerque policeman would ever spot it.

Tristan's garage opening gadget was on the passenger seat, and my old plastic warranty card was in my shirt pocket, the same one that had once briefly held twenty-five crisp hundred-dollar bills. Geronimo was in the back seat.

The first house was number 100. I parked on the street, connected the leash to Geronimo's collar, led him up to the door, and told him to ring the doorbell.

He didn't understand, so I pointed to the button and made encouraging remarks like, "Get it boy," and "Come on, up you go."

His primitive canine brain sensed I wanted him to do something, but all he did was just sway from side to side which made his neck look floppy. Finally, he got the general idea and jumped up against the wall. When his paw failed to hit the button after several attempts, I lost patience and was reaching to ring it myself when the door flew open and a big hairy guy with no shirt and a gut hanging over his buckle said, "What the hell's going on?"

"This dog is lost, and I'm trying to return him to his owner."

He had a tattoo of a naked woman on his forearm. Because of his body hair, she looked like a female orangutan with unusually large breasts. He looked at his door.

"The dog scratched my door."

"Uh, yeah. That's why I thought he might belong here. He wanted to get in."

He took a half step towards me. "I should make you repaint it."

"Actually, I'm just a volunteer working for the animal shelter. If you call them, I'm sure they'll send someone out to fix the door." I stepped around him and pretended to be assessing the damage to the door while actually looking inside. As I suspected, it was not where I had done the appraisal.

I decided to wait on 102 until the guy in 100 calmed down and forgot about me. He didn't look like a guy with a good memory.

I went to the other end of the cluster, shortened Geronimo's leash, and rang the bell at 142. A woman with ample lips and dimpled cheeks answer the door and smiled at me. I gave her my story about the lost dog, and she bent down and rubbed Geronimo behind his ears.

While she was petting Geronimo, I looked into her house and ascertained it was not where I had done the appraisal.

"He's adorable," she said, and you could tell he understood what she was saying about him. "I don't own a pet. But if you can't find his owner, I might be interested in adopting him."

"Thanks, I'll keep you in mind," I said and started to leave.

"Wait, don't you want to take my name and number just in case? Or maybe you have a form from the shelter I can fill out?"

"I forgot to bring any forms, but I'll bring one back to you."

"Won't you need my address to do that?"

I glanced at the number on her door.

Her eyes followed mine, and she said, "How stupid of me. You already know it."

Having sized her up as not the brightest *candelaria* on the *paseo*, I told her the dog's tag had a picture of Indian pottery on it when we found him. I asked her if she knew anyone in the neighborhood who collected Indian pots. She said she didn't. She also said the only person she knew in the neighborhood who owned a dog was Darryl Brumby two doors down at number 138 who had a Rottweiler. I thanked her and went to 140.

No one was home.

I skipped 138, the one with the Rottweiler, because I had seen no evidence of a dog when I did the appraisal.

Okay, the real reason I skipped it was because I'm afraid of Rottweilers.

No one answered the door at 136.

134 was answered by a teenage girl who told me her mother was at work. I told her I was trying to find the owner of a lost dog. She asked me what the dog looked like. "Like this," I said, pointing at Geronimo.

"Exactly like that?"

"Pretty much," I said.

"I don't think I've seen another dog like that."

The house had an assortment of tchotchkes on the shelves next to the fireplace.

I drove around to the service drive to examine the two houses where no one had answered the door. The shade on the rear window at 140 was partway up. I peeked through at the shelves. A fish tank and a few odds and ends.

The shade was down at 136. I peeked in the garage. It was empty. I used Tristan's device to open the garage door. Then I waited for several minutes in the Bronco with the engine running. The garage door was noisy as it went up. If anyone was home and came to investigate, I wanted to make a quick getaway.

When no one came, I used my warranty card to loid the back door, doing so as quietly as possible. I stood silently behind the door and listened for any noise from within. Hearing none, I stepped inside, opened the swinging door, and looked at the shelves. Cabbage Patch dolls.

I closed the back door, lowered the garage door, and drove home. I had used up my supply of nerve. The next cluster would have to wait for another day.

26

I was recharging my nerves that evening in Dos Hermanas and telling Susannah about my initial attempt to determine where the reclusive collector lived.

"She actually bought the story that his tags had a picture of an Indian Pot?"

"I was just a friendly volunteer from the animal shelter. Why would I lie to her?"

"You need a better cover story. The rest of the residents of Titanium Trail may not be so gullible."

"Any suggestions?"

"You could be a door-to-door salesman."

"I don't think I'd make a good salesman."

"You run a store, Hubert."

"Yeah, but I don't sell things. I mean, I have things for sell, and if people buy them, that's good. But I don't actually try to *sell* things."

"A retail shop run by a guy who doesn't like to sell things. I have to admit that's a novel business plan."

"It's a lot better than going door to door and trying to talk someone into buying a . . . What would I be selling?"

"You wouldn't be selling anything. It's just a cover story."

"But I'd have to be selling *something*. I can't just say, 'Hi, I'm a door-to-door salesman. Any of your neighbors collect Indian pottery?'"

"You could sell pots! No one's going to buy one of course, but it would give them the chance to tell you if there's a collector in the neighborhood."

"I think I'll stick with the lost dog story."

"Why do you need any kind of story to begin with? I thought you were going to get the address from Whit."

"He wouldn't give it to me."

"How can you steal the pots for him if he won't tell you where they are?"

"He thinks I already know where they are. When I asked him for the address, he said, 'You already know the address. And I'm going to give you some unofficial advice that you never heard from me. Don't go back there.' Then he hung up."

She stared at me while the wheels turned. "Have you figured out why he said that?"

I shook my head and waved for Angie.

"It doesn't sound good," she ventured.

"Yeah. That's why I hid the Cadillac. It's also why I went looking for my copies. I have a really bad premonition about this whole thing."

"Why didn't you just take the Cadillac back and park it in Cantú's garage like you said you were going to do?"

"Because I'm trying to extricate myself from this affair, and it's obvious the car's been hotwired."

"So it's been hotwired. The cops would never connect you with something like that."

"I know that, but your fingerprints are probably all over the car, and if they discover that, they'll know I'm involved."

"They won't need fingerprints to know you had the car. It sat around your shop for several days, and Izuanita will tell them you took her for a ride in it."

"The cops have no reason to know she exists. And if they don't get suspicious about the car to begin with, they won't go asking people if they've seen it near my shop."

"I can see you've been thinking about this. What's our plan?"

"Can you take out the switch you installed and unhotwire the thing?"

"Sure. The switch is just hanging from the ignition wires. It's not like I drilled a hole in the dash. I'll just remove the switch and splice the wires back together."

"And they won't be able to tell it's been hotwired?"

"Not unless they look under the dash at the wires, and why would they do that if they had no reason to?"

I began to relax a little after Susannah explained the hotwire repair. We could return the car to the garage, wipe off the whole thing to remove any fingerprints, and the car couldn't connect me to Cantú or the dead collector. Then I could retrieve my three copies so they couldn't connect me either, and I'd be home free. I'd even be ahead eventually because after the collection had been sorted out by the police, the probate court or whatever, I could quietly sell the copies.

I don't know why I suddenly had such a strong urge to disentangle myself. After all, I had invested a lot of time and effort, recreating my blindfolded ride, staking out Cantú's place, pretending to be a volunteer from the animal shelter and even taking a car for ransom. During all that time I had seen it as an effort to recover my appraisal fee and, with Whit's help, maybe get a large supplement to that fee. But now I was sitting there looking at Susannah across the table and wishing I'd never gotten involved.

Maybe it was Whit thinking I knew the collector's address and warning me not to go there. Maybe it was just nerves from playing the role of a shelter volunteer and loiding my way into someone else's house. I hate doing that. My stomach was knotted up like macramé. Or maybe it was just a premonition.

27

The premonition followed me home and spent the night with me.

Even though weekends are normally Big Breakfast Days for me, I didn't feel like making the effort the next morning, so I walked down to Barela's and had two *churros* with black coffee. As is always the case on Saturday mornings, the place was packed. Then it hit me—most people don't work on Saturdays.

I packed a picnic lunch and put it, Tristan's magic garage door opener and Martin's book on Einstein in the Bronco and drove to *Casitas del Bosque.* I took Geronimo along, but this time he wasn't part of my disguise.

I nudged the Bronco slowly over the curb and parked up against the bank of the irrigation canal that ran parallel to Platinum Place just where it intersected Titanium Trail. I set up my lawn chair under a large catalpa and tied Geronimo to the tree.

It was a hot summer day, but the dry desert air was cool under the tree, and I had a good view of the entire street. I spent about an hour drinking coffee from a thermos and reading about the uncertainty principle. Then Geronimo and I went behind a willow thicket to do what a dog does on three legs and a man on two.

After we came back, several cars came by and a couple of them gave me a quizzical look. It occurred to me that perhaps the area under the trees was part of the communal property of *Casitas del Bosque*, so I decided to check with the nice lady at *casita numero* 142 to make sure I wasn't going to be asked to leave by the neighborhood patrol.

When she opened the door and saw it was me, she said with a smile, "Did you come back to tell me I can adopt him?"

"Uh, no. It's too soon."

She looked disappointed.

"We give the owner a certain number of days to claim the animals before we allow them to be adopted."

"How many days?"

"Uh, I'm not certain."

"Oh, right. You told me you're new at this."

"Right. The reason I stopped by was I wanted to ask you if you thought it would be okay if the two of us had a picnic over there under the trees."

"That would be great. Just let me put on some shoes," she said and left me standing there like an idiot as she went back into the house.

I looked at Geronimo and said, "You understood that the two of us meant you and me, right?"

He nodded.

She was gone so long I began to suspect she'd lost her shoes, but she finally came back to the door with shoes, lemonade and *bizcochitos*.

After we shared the lunch I'd brought, I let Geronimo off his leash and he went for a swim in the canal. He plopped down in the dirt afterwards and woke up an hour later looking like the company mascot for a regiment of those mud soldiers they dug up in China. Or a clay anteater.

When my companion from number 142 with ample lips and dimpled cheeks saw Geronimo's condition, she went back to her house and returned with an old blanket. I took the dog back to the canal and threw him in. He paddled around for a few minutes. I winched him out, but this time I held the leash tight and kept him off the dirt.

Miss Lips, as I had come to think of her, spread the blanket around the trunk of the catalpa like the apron around a Christmas tree. I tied Geronimo to the tree with the leash shortened enough that he couldn't get off the blanket. After Miss Lips had rubbed his ears a while, he went to sleep.

"What will you do if someone comes along and claims to be the owner?" she asked.

"I'll give him his dog and go back to the shelter."

She looked alarmed. "But what if it's not really the owner?"

I didn't know what to say and I said it.

"It could be a bad person," she said, as if this would help me know what to do.

"You know," she continued, "like someone who does experiments on animals."

"I hadn't thought of that," I admitted.

"Doesn't the shelter have rules about that?"

"I'm not sure. I'm just a volunteer."

"Maybe you need a sign."

"A sign?" I pictured a man claiming ownership of the dog and then a white dove flying by as a sign that the man was not someone who collected animals for evil cosmetic companies to test their products on.

"Yeah, like 'Is this your dog?'" she explained.

"Oh, *that* kind of sign."

"I can cut out the side of a cardboard box and nail it to a tomato stake. We can write on it with a Sharpie."

I couldn't come up with a plausible objection to the sign. After all, if I was trying to find the owner, I could hardly object to a sign that would help me do so. As she walked back to her house, I thought about that old saying about the webs we weave when we lie. I had made up what I thought was a harmless deception to help me find the collector's address, and now I was trapped in it.

When Miss Lips came back, I noticed as she approached that her lips were not the only ample part of her anatomy. She was about as different from Izuanita as a woman could be—short, pudgy, pigeon-toed, and round-faced. Yet attractive in her own way.

"I'm sorry," I said as she sat down next to me, "but I don't know your name."

She smiled at me and said, "I'm Dolly Aguirre."

"I'm Hubert Schuze, but my friends call me Hubie. Is Dolly a nickname?"

"Nope. It's on my birth certificate, Dolly Madison Aguirre. My father taught American history."

"Oh my God! Did he teach at Albuquerque High?"

"Yep. And you're going to tell me you had him as a teacher, right?"

"I did. Frank Aguirre, right?"

She smiled and nodded.

"Is he still teaching?"

"Oh no, he retired years ago. In fact, he lives with me. You want to come over and say hello?"

Oops. There was that deceptive web thing again. Oh well, it's not like Mr. Aguirre was going to call the animal shelter to check up on whether I volunteered there. And what would he do if he found out I told a white lie to his daughter, go back and change my grade to an F?

I told her I thought I should stay at my post in case the owner happened to drive by, but that I'd like to talk to her dad another time.

We sat together on the blanket and passed a pleasant Saturday afternoon talking, eating *bizcochitos* and drinking lemonade. I also watched the comings and goings of the residents of Titanium Trail.

It turned out Dolly also had her father as a teacher. It had proved awkward for her and for the other students who always assumed she didn't have to work for her grades. She told me she did in fact get a break from her dad on her grade. He gave her a D even though she thought she had failed.

Dolly had been at Albuquerque High as a freshman when I was a senior, but she didn't remember me, probably because I didn't play sports. The only people you can remember almost thirty years after you leave high school are the girls you dated—or in my case, the ones I *wanted* to date—and the sports stars. I didn't remember her either, but then who pays attention to freshmen?

I continued to keep one eye on the comings and goings of her neighbors while we talked, and around five she said she needed to check up on her father. Then she asked me if I'd like to have Sunday dinner at her house the next evening and get a chance to visit with her dad.

I wondered whether she was asking me for a date and hesitated briefly before accepting her invitation.

I stayed under the catalpa until around seven then drove home. I put Geronimo out in the patio, put a bookmarker in Martin's book on page fifteen and made myself a large plate of *nachos* with fresh roasted jalapeños on top.

The house I had honed in on was number 130. No one had come and gone all day, the air conditioner wasn't on, and no light had shone through any window at any point during the day. I was there again now that it was getting dark. I sat in the Bronco as day turned to night and lights flickered on everywhere except number 130. An hour after full dark, I drove slowly to the garage and opened it. I carried a footstool in and loided the door to the house.

I stood motionless and listened. Nothing.

By this time, I knew the floor plan like I lived there. I also knew the house was empty. The air was hot and stale. I turned left as I entered the door from the garage, pushed open the swinging door, turned right and then looked right to the shelves.

The moon was not yet up, but even with the faint ambient light I could see the pots. I used the footstool to reach the copy on the top shelf. I took it out to the Bronco and put it in a box I'd brought for that purpose. I pushed newspaper around it to pad it for the ride back to Old Town. I repeated those steps for the other two copies except for the footstool part.

I drove home slowly, avoiding potholes and sudden stops.

When I bought the ancient adobe I now call home, the rear portion had a hundred year backlog of deferred maintenance. My remodel included removing everything down to the original adobe bricks and putting plaster over every square inch of wall except for two expansion joints.

But they aren't there for expansion purposes. They are actually the edges of a door that swings open when I turn and press the wall sconce. Behind the door is my secret hiding place where I put the three copies.

28

The wooden hand-carved sign outside the Church reads, "*Iglesia de San Felipe de Neri—Fundada 1706.*"

The *fundador* was Don Francisco Cuervo y Valdez, the man who also founded our fair city. One brochure says the following about the statue of Cuervo y Valdez that sits at the entrance to Old Town: "The 12' 6" equestrian bronze, dedicated April 1988, depicts the founder of Albuquerque and his horse in authentic dress."

Having seen the thing many times, I can assure you the horse is not wearing a dress, authentic or otherwise.

Cuervo y Valdez originally gave the name of San Francisco Xavier to the Church. But after he named the city in honor of the *Duque de Alburquerque*, the *Duque* ordered the name of the Church changed to *San Felipe de Neri* in honor of King Philip of Spain. We don't know who ordered the first "r" dropped from the spelling of Albuquerque.

I also don't know of any connection between the Saint and the King other than their name, and I don't think the King was named for the Saint because there are eighteen different saints named Philip or Filipe, and the one called Neri was an Italian noted for his sense of humor.

The King, on the other hand, had little sense of humor. He had the city of Xàtiva burned to the ground when they lost a battle, and then he renamed the city after himself. Today, a portrait of Philip V still hangs in the local museum there, but it is deliberately displayed upside down.

I like the fact that the sign in front of Old Town's church is in Spanish. While national political debates rage over things like "English First" and "Bilingualism," Albuquerqueans live in a city where Spanish and English peacefully coexist. One might even say lazily.

The policy debates are inane. People who live in America eventually learn English no matter what their native tongue. People who live in Albuquerque usually learn Spanish, even if English is their first language.

But nobody worries about it. If you don't pick up Spanish, you miss out on much of the charm of the city, but it's your loss and there are no language police.

I was contemplating adding to Schuze's Anthropological Premises a new SAP on the topic of language when mass finally ended and Father Groaz eventually made his way out to find me sitting on the adobe wall as I often do on Sunday afternoons.

"Gud afternoon, Youbird," he greeted me.

"Hi, Father. Can I have a word with you?"

"Yass," he said and then smiled. "Do you want to make confession?"

"I'm not Catholic, Father."

"I know thot, Youbird, so we can make it informal here on the sidewalk."

He sat down beside me.

"I'm worried about Miss Gladys," I told him.

"You do not trust her new suitor."

"You know about him, huh?"

"Yass. Several people have mentioned this to me. Bot no one has said he has done something bad to her."

"Yet," I said.

He leaned his head back in thought and stroked his bushy beard. "God made man and woman to be together. He also gave us each the ability to choose. We should not judge Mr. Fister. And we must not assume that Miss Gladys is gullible old woman."

"That's why I haven't said anything to her. I didn't want her to feel patronized. But I also don't want her to be hurt."

"If you interfere, you will certainly hurt her. If you do not, she may still be hurt, but is not certain. Better to have romance and risk a hurt than to have a hurt inflicted on you by a well-meaning friend."

We sat in silence while I thought about it. I felt certain the good father was right. But I also felt certain that T. Morgan Fister was up to no good. To not interfere seemed wrong. To interfere seemed worse. I was like one of those subatomic particles—uncertain.

I had a meeting with Chris, so I strolled back to my shop and found him waiting. I apologized for being late and told him I'd been at *San Felipe de Neri* talking to the priest. Chris seemed pleased that a church in New Mexico was named after a saint from his hometown of Florence, and he told me he had studied Neri's teachings, which included a simple motto—Be good, if you can.

I offered Chris a beer. He asked if I had red wine. I apologized that I did not. He ended up with water. He started telling me more about Neri, and between the subject matter and his fractured locutions, I admit my attention drifted.

The Cadillac was where no Albuquerque Policeman or Highway Patrolman could spot it, and the three copies were safely tucked away in my secret compartment.

Yet I was still worried. I needed time to think it through just to make sure there wasn't some further precaution I needed to take, and I wondered when I could do that because I had promised to have dinner with Dolly Aguirre and her father that evening.

So I was wishing Chris would leave, and I stopped correcting his English because that only prolonged his visit. And I was uncomfortable that he always sat so close even though Susannah had explained that it was just part of Italian culture.

In fact we were talking about Susannah at one point, so I wasn't surprised when he asked me if I thought he was attractive. I told him he was, and he told me I was, and I assumed he was just being nice and returning the compliment.

And then he leaned over and kissed me passionately on the mouth.

29

Dolly greeted me at the door wearing a yellow blouse over a long green skirt. She looked like a plump sunflower.

It was a good look, casual but dressed for dinner, and it almost matched my choice of a yellow cotton button-down shirt over chinos. No jacket or tie.

I brought a present for her father, David McCullough's acclaimed recent biography of John Adams. Bringing nothing would've been bad manners, and I'd rejected flowers because they would reinforce the ambiguity of the event. She hadn't actually asked me for a date. But I hadn't asked her on a picnic either, and look what happened.

Frank Aguirre looked exactly as I imagined he would, the same face that evidenced a Native American grandparent or two, now wrinkled and topped by silver hair, but the same intelligent eyes.

"It's great to see you again after all these years, Mr. Aguirre," I said to him after Dolly led me into the living room.

"Call me Frank," he said, but I didn't.

"I remembered how much you loved reading," I said and thrust the book out awkwardly.

He smiled and held it with two hands as if trying to assay its intellectual heft. Then he looked up at me sharply, "How did you know I haven't read this?"

I looked towards Dolly and he smiled.

She asked me if I'd like a drink before dinner, and I asked Mr. Aguirre what he was having.

"Decaffeinated coffee," he said with disgust. "Doctor's orders."

Dolly said she was having wine. I knew it wouldn't have bubbles, so I chose the decaf.

The interior décor of the Aguirre home belied the exterior, which was like every other house on the street. The beige carpet had been replaced with hardwood floors covered here and there by worn Navajo rugs. The walls were the color of cantaloupe with a gouache artfully applied to make the gypsum board appear to be genuine plaster. Non-structural ceiling beams had been added by a skilled carpenter.

The furniture was rustic campaign, the chairs and sofa cushions covered in various brocades, and the parchment-shaded lamps cast a candlelight glow. Unfortunately, the cream-colored window shade remained. The overall feel was slightly kitschy but mostly homey, and we sat and talked while the chicken roasted, the house redolent with garlic and rosemary.

Dolly adored her father and proudly told me he'd been the first teacher at Albuquerque High to receive a doctorate. Politeness required me to ask about it, and he told me he had written his dissertation at UNM on how U.S. immigration policy between 1864 and 1893 affected the labor market of that period. Evidently the most important step to ensure a successful dissertation is to define the topic so narrowly that no one else has written on precisely that subject.

Not knowing enough about the topic to ask an intelligent question, I asked instead what the significance of the specific time period was.

"1864 was the first Congressional attempt to get a handle on the topic. They passed a law creating a Commissioner of Immigration and authorizing contracts wherein would-be immigrants could exchange a pledge of wages for transportation to the U.S. The end of the period, 1885, marked the passage of the first contract labor law, effectively bringing policy full circle."

I nodded as if that meant something to me, and Mr. Aguirre broke into a smile.

"Even more boring than my American history classes, right?"

"I liked your classes," I said honestly, "but I don't remember us discussing immigration policy."

"I had to stick to the approved curriculum. Can you still name all the presidents and their dates in office?"

"No."

"I wouldn't think so. And who cares when Franklin Pierce was president?"

"There was a president named Franklin Pierce?"

He and Dolly laughed.

"The theory in the public schools," he explained, "is that social studies prepare you for responsible citizenship. If all the students I taught and all the students all the other history teachers taught over the last thirty years had studied immigration policy instead of memorizing the presidents, we might be having a more intelligent national debate about what to do about illegal immigration."

My mother advised me not to discuss religion or politics at the dinner table, but that evening we discussed little else. Aguirre's position was that immigration policy is driven by labor considerations. When the unions have their way, immigration is restricted and there is less competition for jobs and therefore better pay. When capitalists have their way, immigration is encouraged as a source of cheap labor. It reminded me of the stories Emilio told me about the *Bracero* program. When I mentioned that to Mr. Aguirre, I was surprised to find that he supported the reinstatement of such a program despite the fact that he was basically a Marxist on the labor issue.

Aguirre excused himself shortly after dinner. Dolly refused my offer to help with the dishes, insisting instead that we move to the living room for coffee and dessert. The latter was an excellent flan, the former a thin brew. Even though we didn't remember each other from high school, reminiscences came easily because we had in common a few friends and many experiences at the old AHS before it was abandoned and later turned into condos.

When I finally took my leave, she walked me to the door. When I opened it and turned to say goodnight, there ensued an awkward moment of silence. I moved my hand out in a deliberately uncertain manner that could be interpreted as either the start of a handshake or a friendly embrace. She took my hand in both of hers, tugged me gently towards her, and gave me a demure kiss.

"Will I see you again?" she asked.

"I'd like that," I answered.

Another brief moment of silence, but not quite so awkward.

"In that case," she said, "maybe we should have a proper goodnight kiss."

And we did, except that improper might have been a better description of it.

When it was over, she said goodnight and I went home.

30

Having spent an alcohol-free evening with Dolly and her father, I decided a nightcap was in order, and no one will be surprised that I selected Gruet *Blanc de Noir*.

The bottle was already in the fridge. A champagne flute was in the freezer. The green chile caramel truffles were in the cupboard. Cocopotamus—an artisanal chocolate kitchen here in Albuquerque—calls them "Hulk." I don't know why. They aren't large, but they are delicious, probably because the green chile is from Hatch.

I settled in with the Gruet and the truffles to do some serious thinking.

I had experienced two very interesting kisses that day. Chris was a handsome devil, but Dolly was definitely a better kisser. I wasn't offended by Chris' kiss, although I would have avoided it had I seen it coming. I don't find homosexuality abhorrent nor do I think gays are deviants. Chris likes men. I like women. So the problem wasn't Chris—it was Susannah.

I wondered if I could put a positive "spin" on it as they say these days. "Hey Susannah, I've got good news. You know how you were wondering why Chris hasn't tried to put a move on you. Well, you won't have to worry about that anymore because . . ."

Then I thought about not telling her. Just let her figure it out. Miss Gladys could handle T. Morgan and Susannah could deal with Chris. It wasn't my place to butt in. This approach had the *imprimatur* of the Roman Catholic Church. Or at least of Father Groaz, a man who is wiser than I am and also a lot holier.

I guided my thoughts to Dolly. She had a cute round face, a creamy complexion, and lovely long lashes. She was a pleasant, easygoing person with a good sense of humor, and she liked Geronimo. She didn't set my heart to pounding like Izuanita did, but I did feel a little pitty-pat when we kissed. Her full lips felt terrific, not to mention the other parts of her anatomy that she squeezed against me when we kissed.

I didn't know where I stood with Izuanita. I might just as well tell her I was abducted by aliens as to let her know I viewed her romantically. In all likelihood I was to her just an odd but mildly entertaining shopkeeper she happened to meet.

My mind kept going back to Susannah. I knew it was not my place to tell her about Chris, but my heart didn't agree, and the longer I thought about it, the more I came to believe she would be disappointed in me if I didn't tell her.

So I woke up Monday morning determined to tell Susannah that evening at Dos Hermanas, dreading doing so, and knowing I'd spend the whole day obsessing about how to phrase it. But as fate would have it, I spent most of the day in jail.

Whit Fletcher was leaning against the wall across the street when I opened for business. He strolled across the street and said, "You have the right to remain silent. Anything you say may be—" Well, you know how that goes, so I won't repeat the entire Miranda warning.

After he read me my rights, he said, "I had a hunch you knew that stiff you said you couldn't identify. What I never suspected was that you killed him."

"That's ridiculous," I replied.

"That's what I said when the report came back from the crime lab. Schuze is a pot thief, he don't murder people. That's what I told 'em. But evidence is evidence, and my opinion that you couldn't kill anybody even if you wanted to ain't evidence. It wouldn't even be allowed in court seeing as how I'm not a shrink. So even though I know you don't have the *cajones* to kill anyone, there's nothing I can do but take you downtown and wish you luck."

"What evidence?"

"Your fingerprints are on the glass that had the poison in it. Didn't it occur to you to wipe the glass off, Hubert? If you'd done that, I wouldn't be arresting you."

Half of my brain was panicking and picturing scenes from prison life, but the other half was thinking. "Was it a pilsner glass?"

"What's that?"

"A type of beer glass, tall and shaped like an ice cream cone."

Whit shook his head in disappointment. "First you forget to wipe off the glass, then you admit to knowing what the glass is after I already Mirandized you. I always figured you was smarter than that."

"I know what the glass is because I saw it when I was at his house."

"This just gets worse and worse for you. Maybe you should shut up until you talk to your lawyer."

"No, listen to me. I went there to give him an estimate on his pot collection. That glass and a bottle of beer were sitting on the coffee table. After I finished doing the estimate, he went to get my money and insisted I drink the beer. That's how my prints got on the glass."

"I thought you didn't know his name."

"I didn't. I still don't. The deal was set up by Carl Wilkes."

"The guy who got you to break into the museum?"

"I didn't break in."

"Maybe you should find some new friends."

"There was nothing illegal this time. Carl said there was a pot collector who had decided to sell his collection and needed an appraisal of its value. The collector didn't want me to know his name. So when you asked me at the morgue if I knew the name of the deceased, and I told you I didn't, I was telling the truth."

"But not the whole truth. You coulda said you'd seen him before."

"What good would that have done you? You still wouldn't have known who he was."

"We coulda gone to his house and found out."

"I didn't know where his house was."

"You just told me thirty seconds ago that you was there pricing out his pots."

"I was, but I didn't know where the house was. I was blindfolded when they took me there and when I left."

He stared at me for a few seconds. "Hubert, I don't know whether you're making up a smokescreen or losing your mind."

Then it came to me. "I was framed!"

"Funny how often that happens," he said. "The state pen's got hunnerds of guys who was framed."

"But I really was. Think about it. The guy practically insisted that I drink the beer. In fact, I was afraid he wasn't going to pay me until I did, so I opened the bottle, poured it in the glass—"

"Pilner glass."

"Pilsner. There's an 's.' Anyway, I poured it in the glass and . . ."

I didn't finish the sentence because it hit me that what I was saying didn't make sense. Why would the collector want my prints on the glass? Frames are constructed by murderers so that someone else takes the fall. But the collector wasn't the murderer. He was the *victim*.

31

The only explanation I could come up with as we drove downtown in Whit's unmarked police cruiser was that the collector committed suicide and wanted to make it look like I had killed him.

You're probably wondering why he would do that insofar as he didn't know me and had no reason to shuffle off this mortal coil in such a fashion as to land me in prison. I was wondering the same thing and with much greater urgency.

The best answer I could come up with was life insurance. Maybe he had a big policy and wanted his kids to get the proceeds. Life insurance, for obvious reasons, doesn't pay when the death is self-inflicted. So by making it look like I killed him, he would make sure the insurance paid off.

But that theory had two flaws. First, what sort of person would want his last act on earth to bring grievous harm to an utter stranger? And second, his heirs would get a million dollars worth of pots, not to mention the house and whatever else he owned, so the lack of a life insurance payoff would hardly be a calamity.

Somehow I never mind talking to Whit and telling him things I shouldn't tell a cop who's arresting me. I guess I figure he knows I'm innocent and can help me even though he never says that. But once we arrived at the police station and he turned me over to other people, I did the wise thing and clammed up.

It took almost three hours for them to search me, fill out forms, fingerprint me, and photograph me. The only thing that didn't take long was the questioning session because I told them I wouldn't answer any questions unless my lawyer was present. They let me call him, and then they put me in a cell.

Fortunately, there was only one other occupant, a tall skinny guy who needed about five thousand dollars worth of cosmetic dentistry but didn't look like he could afford so much as a toothbrush. Or would use it if he could. At one point in his life he must have had enough money for a tattoo The letters h-e-l-l were on the back of the first joints of the fingers of his left hand and the letters b-e-n-t were on the right. If he held his hands out in front of him palms down, he could read "hell bent." But as I looked at his hand, I saw tneb lleh.

One of Layton Kent's paralegals finally showed up around one with legal paperwork, perhaps a writ of some sort or maybe bail. I didn't care. I just wanted out. The process to let me out took almost as long as the one to put me in. I haven't stayed in many hotels because I don't like to travel, but I think the Albuquerque Jail could definitely streamline their check-in/check-out process with a little advice from the folks at the famous hotel company founded by Conrad Hilton from the village of San Antonio, New Mexico.

The paralegal, an attractive young lady with perfect posture and a pleasing smile, drove me to Layton's club in his Rolls Royce. As you may have heard me explain, Layton has an office somewhere, but he seldom uses it. He spends most of his day at his table that overlooks the 18th green at his club. He doesn't play golf or take any other form of exercise, and he looks like a man who spends a great deal of time at a dining table.

He must weigh close to three hundred pounds, but he doesn't look fat. He looks big, of course, but he doesn't seem blubbery. His face is large and its transition to his neck ill-defined, but the whole area is without wrinkles. His hair is precisely cut, his nails perfectly manicured, his clothes stylish.

The word that comes to mind is sleek. Not sleek like a cheetah, sleek like a whale. Very large but still sleek, the only bulge—and I'm just guessing here—being his wallet, which must be enormous.

He is widely considered to be the most influential man in Albuquerque. He knows everyone who is anyone, and quite a few people like me who are no one. His lovely wife, Mariella, is the *Grande Dame* of Albuquerque society. She isn't just *on* the A list—she draws it up. She is reputed to be a descendent of the Duke who gave our fair city its unusual name. This seems unlikely. Royalty didn't travel overseas in those days. Considering what it must have been like to cross the Atlantic in a wooden ship about eighty feet long, who could blame them?

Layton's practice centers on creating legal ways for rich people to get richer and avoid paying taxes on their riches. His client list includes most wealthy Albuquerqueans and a lot of other lawyers. They like to use him because he is not seen as a competitor. He runs his practice with a bevy of paralegals and secretaries but no other attorneys. And he stoops to criminal law only when a current client requires it.

I seem to require it more than his other clients, and I'm sure he would have dropped me from his list the first time I was accused of murder had it not been for Mariella. She is a collector of rare Native American pottery, and I am her personal dealer.

Layton was wearing a white linen suit, a pair of tan and white saddle oxfords, a silk shirt the color of the fine tan leather on the saddle of the shoes and a sage-colored knit tie. He could have passed for Sydney Greenstreet playing in a movie written by F. Scott Fitzgerald.

He laced his manicured fingers on the table and sat motionless as I told him the whole story, starting with the blindfolded ride, backtracking to the three visits of Segundo Cantú and the reappearance of Carl Wilkes then all the shenanigans on Titanium Trail.

"You left out an important detail," he said after I finished.

"I have heard your explanation of why the client has to tell the lawyer everything," I replied, "and that's what I did."

"And the name of the person you are charged with murdering?"

"I have no idea."

His eyebrows rose without his brow furrowing. I don't know how that's possible. Maybe he's had plastic surgery and the skin is so taut on his face that the upward motion of the lifting brows is transferred all the way over his head. Every time he does that trick I want to walk around behind him and see if the back of his neck is wrinkled.

He didn't say anything, so I did. "Remember I told you about Whit making me go to the morgue to identify a corpse? I knew who it was—the collector—but I didn't know his name."

"I understand that you didn't know it then. But surely they must have told you the name when you were arrested."

I shook my head.

Layton raised one hand and the attractive paralegal came to the table with her briefcase.

"Our copy of Mr. Schuze's arrest warrant, Jenny."

She retrieved it from the briefcase and handed it to him.

Layton smiled. "You probably think I retain you as a client because Mariella is fond of you."

I nodded.

"That is a factor. But there is another. You are the most incompetent client in the annals of jurisprudence, and I enjoy the challenge of representing you."

I wanted to tell His Pompousness that I didn't give a damn about being a competent client, but discretion required me to remain silent.

"You have been arrested and processed without even knowing whom you are accused of killing. It is not, as you surmised, the anonymous pot collector. It is another player in the narrative you gave me—Segundo Cantú."

I felt like I was in free fall. I grabbed the table and took deep breaths. After the spinning sensation subsided, I started thinking, and I remembered Whit's exact words from that morning.

"It can't be Cantú," I told Layton. "After Whit read me my rights, he said, 'I had a hunch you knew that stiff you said you couldn't identify. What I never suspected was that you killed him.' So it has to be the collector."

Layton thought for a few seconds. "There are only two possible explanations. One is that Detective Fletcher made a mistake. I reject that possibility *prima facie*. Fletcher is a Philistine, but he is by no means incompetent. Thus, we must accept the second possibility."

"And that is?"

"The collector was also named Segundo Cantú."

32

"So segundo cantú . . ." Susannah started. Then she hesitated and evidently decided she needed to clarify. "The young one," she said, "the one you didn't kill—"

"I didn't kill the older one either."

"I know that, Hubie, but for now we have to go with the police's version. Anyway, I was going to say that the young one must be Segundo Cantú, Junior. So that makes him Second the Second!"

"Maybe he's not a junior," I ventured. "Maybe they just happened to have the same name."

"Right. Two guys named Segundo Cantú, and one of them just happens to ask the other one—who lives on the same street by the way—to deliver his pots down to Spirits in Clay because there's a guy down there in Old Town named Segundo Schuze who can copy them."

"Except I'm not named Segundo."

"It wouldn't be any weirder if you were. They have to be father and son. And that should help us figure out who did it."

She was in her element, a real live murder mystery. She loved it.

I was also in the murder mystery. Unfortunately, I was the suspect, and I hated it.

I have a tendency to drink too much when I'm under pressure, so I was nursing my margarita to avoid that pitfall. Susannah kept glancing at my glass because she was ready for a second—or maybe I should say a *segundo*—and we always order refills simultaneously.

"A girl could die of thirst waiting for you to finish that thing," she finally said and then added, "You drink. I'll talk. They have a good case against you. First, you admitted going to his house. Second, your prints are on the murder weapon—"

"A glass isn't a mur—"

"You drink. I'll talk. Your prints are on the glass that had the poison that killed him. I'd say that's a murder weapon. Third, you lied to Whit at the morgue—"

"I didn't—"

"You drink. I'll talk. You didn't tell a lie, but you also didn't tell him you had seen the guy, something an innocent person would have done. Fourth—"

"I am innocent and . . ." I saw her eyes narrow and held up a palm. "I know, I know. I'll drink, you talk."

"Where was I? Oh, right, number four. Fourth, you have a motive—he swiped your pay for the appraisal. Face it, Hubert—it looks bad. The only way to get you out of this fix is for us to find the real murderer. And that should be easy."

I took a small sip.

"Well?" she said.

"I'm drinking, you're talking."

"Take another sip, then you can talk."

I did. Then I asked her why she thought it would be easy to find the real murderer.

"Because," she explained, "you already know so much about the case. The son brought copies to you. You broke into his house—"

"I didn't—"

"I know you say it's not breaking in when you don't steal anything, but the police don't look at it that way. Keep drinking. You saw his house. You stole his car—"

"You hotwired it."

"Right, but you're the one who drove it away. And you kept it, which turns out to be a good thing because maybe there's a clue in it. And you saw the collection and discovered your copies in it. You saw that house when you did the appraisal and again when you broke in and stole the copies."

"They were *my* copies," I said in exasperation.

"No," she countered, "they were *his* copies because *he* paid for them. And finally, you know someone is trying to frame you because of the lengths Cantú Senior went to get your prints on the glass."

I finally finished my drink, and Susannah signaled the long-limbed Angie for another round. Angie has a triangular face with a wide mouth and the shiniest dark brown eyes I've ever seen. If they were stars, they'd rate at least a magnitude five on Ptolemy's luminosity scale.

I took a very small sip of my second margarita to make sure it was as good as the first. It was better.

"The fingerprint thing really confuses me," I admitted. I told her about my life insurance theory, but she dismissed that as ridiculous, and I can't say I disagreed with her.

She said, "I think it's safe to assume the murderer didn't say to Cantú Senior, 'I'm planning to poison you, so make sure to get Schuze's prints on one of your glasses so I can blame it on him.' But Cantú did make sure to get your prints, so the only explanation that makes sense is that the murderer convinced Cantú to get your prints for some other reason."

"Like what?"

"I don't know, Hubie. When we figure out who the murderer is, we can ask him."

"Okay, who's the murderer?"

"Primero Cantú," she said without hesitation.

"Huh?"

"If there's a Segundo, there must be a Primero. And the oldest child inherits, so he killed his father to get the pots."

"And how do we prove he did it? And before we do that, how do we find him?"

"Do I have to do all the work?"

We kicked it around for the rest of the evening, and she did end up doing all the work because I had nothing to offer. All I knew was I didn't kill Cantú and I had no clue who did.

33

The first person through my door when I opened the shop the next morning was Carl Wilkes.

I was not happy to see him.

"You didn't kill Segundo Cantú, did you?" he asked.

"No, did you?"

"No. And whoever did took an unnecessary risk. If he wanted Cantú dead, he didn't have to poison him. All he had to do was wait."

I dragged my stool around to his side of the counter and he sat down on it. He'd always worn fitted clothes when I'd seen him before, but that morning he was wearing a loose-fitting safari shirt with a vented yoke, loose cuffs, and two patch pockets with tortoiseshell buttons. He would have been right at home in the Kalahari.

I poured us both a cup of Bustelo, and he said it was better than what I'd given him before.

"That's because it had been steeping all day the first time."

He nodded and took another sip.

There was a long silence before he finally spoke. "I met Segundo Cantú at a clinic where we were both taking treatments."

I said nothing. He sipped more coffee.

"He had metastasized melanoma. He was being treated with proluekin. It wasn't working. He had a few months left at best."

"Is that why he wanted to sell his pots?"

Carl shrugged. "That would be my guess, but I didn't ask him."

Another long silence.

"So why are you telling me this?"

"I saw in the paper this morning that you'd been arrested for his murder. I thought maybe this information might be helpful to you."

"He take you on as agent?"

He nodded.

"You find any likely buyers?"

"I was just starting to ask around when he died."

"So now what?"

He shrugged again. It seemed to be an effort. "I guess the estate gets the pots unless he left them to a museum or something. If the estate gets them, maybe they'd keep me as agent. He has two children."

"Let me guess. Their names are Primero and Segundo."

"I know one child is named after the father, so he's Segundo. I don't know the other name, but I'd wager it isn't Primero. Anyway, I'd like to ask Segundo about selling his father's collection, but I can't find him."

"A lot of that going around," I replied.

"Why do they think you killed him?"

"My prints were on the glass with the poison in it."

"Shouldn't you have wiped off your prints after adding the poison?"

"I didn't add any poison."

"I know that. You're not a murderer. What I meant was wouldn't the police realize you would have wiped off your prints? If your prints were on the glass, the logical thing to assume is they were there innocently."

"They were, and I told them that. I told them I was doing an appraisal, and Cantú gave me a beer."

"So it was just bad luck that the poisoner used the glass with your prints on it."

"Yeah, but the police aren't buying that."

After Wilkes left, I sat down on the stool he'd vacated and thought about what he had said. Maybe he was right. Maybe I wasn't framed. Maybe Cantú didn't wash his dishes, and it was just bad luck that my prints were still on the glass when the murderer put the poison in it. That certainly made more sense than my insurance theory of Cantú committing suicide and making it looked like I murdered him. And I couldn't think of anyone else with a motive to frame me.

Maybe it was just bad luck. And maybe some good luck as well. After all, if Cantú's kitchen hygiene was that bad, I was lucky not to have contracted salmonella, strep or jungle rot just from the stuff on his pilsner glass. Well, maybe not jungle rot. It's probably too dry in Albuquerque for that.

Then a thought came to me that I might have some very good luck indeed, and I called Layton Kent. He agreed it was a good thought and said he would act on it immediately.

34

Geronimo wanted to go for a drive the next morning, so I took him out to the Bronco, and the two of us drove the nine miles to Martin Seepu's pueblo.

We found him halter-breaking a roan foal in a corral. Geronimo kept glancing at the horse and then back at me as if I was going to tell him what it was.

"You want that animal trained," said Martin, "he needs to get in line behind the horse."

"He came ready-trained."

"Yeah. That's why he's on a leash."

"I only keep him leashed to protect your livestock. He's ferocious."

Geronimo looked up at me quizzically.

Martin pulled the foal close to him, put one muscular arm around its neck and removed the halter with his free hand. When Martin released his grip, the foal trotted gingerly away.

We walked over to the tack room where Martin had coffee in a dented aluminum percolator on a hot plate.

"What's his name?"

"Geronimo."

"Let me guess. Because he flew into your patio like a paratrooper?"

"Exactly. And also because he's ferocious."

"Right."

"You got some spare time?"

He nodded.

"I need to move that car back into town. Can you follow me in the Bronco?"

"Where's the animal going to ride?"

"With me?"

"Okay, I'll do it."

"I also need you to fix the ignition switch."

"What's wrong with it?'

"It was hotwired."

He stared at me. "I didn't think you could do that, paleface."

"Susannah."

"Ah. Do I want to know why?"

"Probably not."

I drove to 183 Titanium Trail, used Tristan's device for the . . . I lost count of how many times. I know I told him I was only going to use it once, but the circumstances kept shifting.

I wiped down every square inch of the Cadillac inside and out with an old towel while looking all around to make sure I hadn't accidentally dropped anything like a gasoline receipt—the thing was a real guzzler—that would identify me. Martin's repair of the ignition wiring was invisible, so everything was back to normal.

Almost. There were several hundred new miles on the odometer, electrical tape on the ignition wires, and the top was down because I couldn't figure out how to get it back up. So when Cantú next saw his car, he'd be pretty certain someone had been driving it. I just hoped he wouldn't be able to figure out who.

I was about to leave when I remembered Susannah saying there might be clues in the car—which I thought was a real long shot—but I looked for some just in case.

Susannah tells me that crime scene investigation is all the rage on television these days. I picture Sherlock Holmes bending over a corpse with his magnifying glass. Holmes' magnifying glass, that is. The corpse probably wouldn't have one.

As I see it, the problem with looking for clues is that nothing is a clue *per se*. A bottle cap is just a bottle cap. It doesn't become a clue until you notice it's the cap from a brand of ale sold only in Gurgisstad and you see a laundry mark on the lining of the corpse's coat in Cyrillic characters, and you know Gurgisstad uses that alphabet, and so on. I guess it works well in fiction.

Yes, I noticed the red stain on the back seat armrest. Lipstick? A drool from someone enjoying a cherry Lifesaver? How the hell would I know? And even if I did, how would I know whether it was a clue? And if it was a clue, how would I know what it meant?

So I gave up looking for clues, closed the garage door and took Martin home. On the way, he brought up the uncertainty principle again, and I told him I just couldn't bring myself to accept it.

"That's because you're a linear-thinking European," he said.

"Probably."

"The European world view contains a presupposition that there are only two sorts of actions, those brought about by the laws of nature and those brought about by intelligent beings."

I glanced at him quizzically and then back at the road.

"A lodestone points north because of magnetism. People look north because they choose to."

"And your point is?"

He didn't look at me as he spoke, just stared out through the windshield. "I'm explaining why you can't accept the uncertainty principle. You think subatomic particles should follow some law."

"And Indians look at it differently?"

"Not just Indians. All native peoples believe the universe is spiritual. That mountain has a spirit," he said, pointing out the window. "Rocks have spirits, trees have spirits . . ."

He was looking around for a tree to point at but couldn't find one. Hey, it's the desert.

"Okay, everything has a spirit," I said, "How does that relate to uncertainty?"

"If you have a spirit, you can choose. Subatomic particles have spirits. They don't always follow a given path for the same reason people don't always follow a given path. They choose not to do so."

"So that mountain could choose to move closer to the river?"

He disregarded my sarcasm. "Yes. It could *choose* to, but there are some choices it can't implement, just like you might choose to fly, but you can't do it because it's not one of your capabilities. Mountains can't move, people can't fly, subatomic particles can't photosynthesize. But they can choose a path. And we know that because we can't predict where they will go."

To the tune from *Porgy and Bess*, I sang:

Mountain can't move
People can't fly
Subatomic particles
Can't photosynthesize
Can't help loving that man of mine

"Your theory sounds ridiculous," I said

"Not as ridiculous as your singing."

"Agreed. And your logic makes sense," I acknowledged.

He nodded.

An hour or two after I finally got back to Old Town, one of Layton's paralegals called to fill me in on the progress they had made. After my call, Layton had called the Chief of Police and asked him to have the crime lab run a test based on the idea I told him about the day before. The test had shown what I had hoped, and Layton had managed to have an emergency hearing scheduled for the next morning where he was going to petition the court to void my arrest warrant. He was confident the petition would be granted by Judge Aragon.

Needless to say, I was feeling great. The Cadillac was back where I found it with little possibility of being connected to me. The murder charge was likely to be dropped. And I could sell the three copies I had retrieved and get at least five thousand each for them and maybe even more if some unsuspecting buyer thought they were genuine. Either way, it was a lot more than the measly twenty-five hundred appraisal fee I had lost.

The only thing I had to worry about was starvation. I hadn't eaten anything all day except for coffee and a cinnamon *churro*.

And just on cue, Miss Gladys Claiborne appeared at my door with her notorious wicker picnic basket. I was so hungry, even one of her Casseroles of Doom was a welcome sight.

It turned out to be "veggie and grits." For some reason I can't explain, I seem unable to resist asking her to explain these dishes. Hearing how they're made only results in their being even harder to stomach, but I always ask.

"Veggies and grits," she began, obviously proud that I had asked, "starts with a package of frozen Brussels sprouts."

I must have made a face at that news because she assured me that even people who don't like Brussels sprouts (there are people who do?) love this dish.

"You cover the bottom of the casserole dish with the Brussels sprouts slit in half longways and cover those with instant grits. Then you sprinkle Bacos over the grits, cover that with chopped green onions, pour in two cans of cream of celery soup and one can of chicken broth, cover it with about a quarter of an inch of Monterrey Jack cheese, and bake it till it bubbles."

"What's a baco?" I asked with trepidation.

"I swan, Mr. Schuze. Are you going to stand there and tell me you've never had Bacos?"

"I don't know if I have," I admitted.

"They come in a jar right there with the other spices."

"It's a spice? What does it taste like?"

She shook her head in amazement at my ignorance. "They taste like bacon, what else would imitation bacon bits taste like?"

"I see," I said, although I didn't. How can bacon be a spice?

Some of Miss Gladys' concoctions have proven to be quite toothsome, as she might say, but I must admit that, even as hungry as I was, veggie and grits was not one of them. The Brussels sprouts were . . . well, Brussels sprouts. There is no way to conceal their taste despite the fact that it cries out for concealment.

I know grits are made from hominy, an excellent food that is a key ingredient in one of my favorite dishes, *pozole*. But the process of turning hominy into grits must be akin to what they do with dead horses. In both cases you end up with glue.

Suffice it to say the Bacos were the best part of the dish. I ate enough to be polite then begged off a further helping with the lie that I'd eaten a large lunch at Martin's.

"No wonder your appetite is gone. The food they eat at his pueblo is hotter than Hades." She blushed at the word. "I should have brought you some of the Jell-O mold I made yesterday."

"Did it have crushed pineapple and mini marshmallows?"

"You do seem partial to that one, but no. This one is peach Jell-O with canned Mandarin orange segments and crushed wintermint Life Savers."

"Do tell?" I replied. I couldn't help it.

I got a taste of the Jell-O mold when I walked her back to her shop, and she insisted I come in for dessert. It wasn't bad although the little nuggets of Life Savers were a bit too crunchy in my opinion.

I knew she was wanting to tell me something, so I stuck around when she offered me a glass of sweet tea, a beverage made by putting a dozen tea bags and two cups of sugar in a gallon of boiling water then adding ice when the mixture has seeped and cooled. Strong and sweet.

"Morgan drove me to his house for a special dinner last night."

"Oh? Where does he live?"

"He says he's planning to buy a large house, but for now he's renting."

"Near here?"

"No, a small house on one of those streets named after a metal." She waved a hand to the side. "You know I can't remember addresses or telephone numbers at my age."

"You haven't forgotten anything about cooking."

She smiled. There was a pause. "After the dinner, Morgan asked me to marry him," she said, looking down at the floor as she did so.

"He'd be a fool not to."

She looked up and smiled.

"I'd marry you myself, but you claim I'm too young. You are charming, attractive, and an excellent cook. Any man would be lucky to have you as his wife."

She blushed and waved away my flattery with both hands. "Morgan is not as handsome as you, Mr. Schuze, but he is closer to my own age."

"And handsome in his own way. Rather dashing, I'd say."

"Yes, and a good conversationalist. I have enjoyed his company these past few weeks."

"He dresses well, too," I noted.

"After Mr. Claiborne passed away, I never for a moment thought I'd ever be involved with another man."

"That was a long time ago. I'm certain he would want you to live your life to the fullest."

Her eyes teared up. "He told me that on his deathbed."

I fumbled for my handkerchief, but she picked one off a stack of them she had for sale and dabbed her eyes.

"I have enjoyed Morgan's attention. I've enjoyed the company of a man again. Not that I don't always enjoy your company, Mr. Schuze, but I mean—well—the company of a man in the romantic sense."

"I understand," I said.

"I will miss that," she said. She smiled at me.

"You turned him down," I said, not as a question.

"I did."

"Then there's still a chance for me."

When she stopped laughing, she said, "I do declare I love your sense of humor." She hesitated for a moment then said, "I always enjoy your flattery, and although we both know that's all it is, please don't stop."

35

Susannah was full of suggestions that evening regarding our plan to solve Segundo Cantú's murder, and she sounded disappointed when I told her we might not have to do that.

"Why?"

"Because Layton is petitioning the judge to throw out the charges against me."

"On what grounds?"

"On the courthouse grounds, I suppose. Where else would he throw them?"

"Groan."

"Sorry, but I'm in a giddy mood. The crime lab tested Cantú's pilsner glass and found my DNA on the rim of the glass."

"So what? You already admitted handling the glass."

"That's why my *fingerprints* were on it. But the DNA on the rim didn't come from my fingers. It came from my saliva."

"Which means you drank from that glass."

"Exactly. And that validates the story I told Fletcher, that I went to Cantú's just to do an appraisal and had a glass of beer."

She was getting excited. It wasn't as good as solving the murder, but at least it was solving a sort of mystery. "And he was alive and well when you left."

"Well, alive anyway. Turns out he was far from well. According to Wilkes, Cantú had metastasized melanoma and had only a few months left to live."

"That makes the murder even more intriguing. But let's get back to your situation first. Drinking from Cantú's glass doesn't prove you didn't poison him. Maybe you were thirsty, put some water in the glass, took a sip and then put the poison in and gave it to Cantú."

"I suppose it could have happened that way, but my story is more probable. Since they have no motive and no witnesses, the glass evidence is just too weak and circumstantial."

"What about the appraisal fee being taken back? That could be a motive."

I shook my head. "First, twenty-five hundred is hardly enough to murder someone for, but even more importantly, they don't know about that."

"You didn't tell them about the missing fee?"

"I told them nothing, sweetheart," I said in my best Bogart imitation.

"Not even close," she said.

We were running low on salsa, so I waved to Angie and she brought another bowlful.

"I have more good news. Miss Gladys spurned T. Morgan Fister."

"Spurned?"

"Yeah. He proposed to her and she turned him down."

"I know what 'spurned' means. It just sounds so old-fashioned."

"She's an old-fashioned woman."

"That she is. Did she say why?"

"No. She said she had enjoyed his company and was going to miss having romance in her life."

"That's sad, Hubie. But at least it tells us something important."

"She knew he was a flimflam man?"

"Yeah. She probably wished he hadn't popped the question and they could have just gone on dating."

"That would be my guess."

"Maybe she'll find someone else."

"I told her I was still available."

"What about Izuanita and Dolly."

"I'm available for them too."

"Cad."

"Now there's an old fashioned word."

36

Martin's cousin, Kennedy, had given me two large butcher-paper-wrapped pieces of a dead deer.

As you may have guessed from that description, I am not fond of venison. I do, however, know one man who can make it not only edible but quite tasty, so the next morning I was in the Bronco with the deer parts as passengers.

I was glad to finally get them out of my refrigerator. They weren't spoiling—they'd been there only three days. But they were spoiling my appetite. And it's awkward to fish around the fridge for a beer with one hand while holding the door open with the other and your head canted away so you can't see what's in there.

It was a beautiful morning with just a faint scent of irrigated land in the air. I drove down the south valley until I reached the small adobe on the unnamed dirt road and found Emilio waiting for me.

"Bienvenido, Señor Uberto."

"Buenos días, Señor Sanchez."

"Consuela waits for us in the garden."

We carried the meat with us around the house and placed it on a large wooden table. Emilio went inside to bring coffee while I greeted Consuela.

"You look good," I told her.

"I pray to the Virgin," she said and crossed herself. "And of course I have a good husband," she added impishly.

We chatted for a while, and I began to wonder if Emilio had to roast and grind the beans before brewing the coffee. When he finally arrived, I understood why it had taken so long. He was carrying a large ceramic bowl with an aromatic slurry of ground *ancho* chiles, brown sugar, apple cider vinegar, fresh crushed oregano, corn oil, ground cumin, freshly pounded cloves and a couple of heads of rough-chopped garlic.

It's called *adobada*, and an old tennis sneaker left in it long enough would be tasty after grilling. It works even better with pork, and it makes venison taste almost as good as beef.

Along with the bowl, Emilio had brought an old wooden-handled knife, and he sat sharpening it on a stone as we enjoyed our coffee. After he'd given me a refill, he began slicing the venison expertly into long strips. After the meat was separated, he broke the bones with a hammer and threw them into the sauce along with the meat so that the marrow would deepen the flavor.

"The meat must remain in the *adobada* overnight, Uberto. But after it is grilled tomorrow, I will bring some to you."

I smiled at him. "That is why I brought it to you."

"It seems like all the men in my life can cook," Consuela said with a pleasant smile.

Despite her assessment of our cooking skills and our offers to display them, Consuela insisted on preparing lunch. Even over the strong scent of the *adobada*, my nose had already informed me there were roasting peppers in the oven. Emilio and I stayed on the patio while Consuela cooked the *chiles rellenos.* They are not on the approved list for heart patients, but so far as I know, I'm in good health, so I had three of them. Any damage they did to my body was offset by the good they did for my soul. We talked and ate and drank, Consuela hot tea, Emilio and I cold Tecates.

37

I arrived back in Old Town a little before four, parked in the alley, and went into my living quarters through the back door. Then I went into my workshop and looked through the peephole into the shop.

Why do I have a peephole from my workshop into the shop? Because if I walk out into the shop and someone is peering in, I have to open up. But if I peek through the hole, I leave my options open. If the person looks like a buyer, I open. If they look like browsers, then they don't have to know I'm on the premises.

The people I saw that afternoon were neither buyers not browsers. They were demonstrators, and they were carrying placards that said, "Immigrants Deserve Justice."

I thought it was bad luck they'd selected my shop as the location for their demonstration. But when a reporter stationed herself in front of my logo and started doing a "stand-up" with her partner aiming a portable camera at her, I realized I was the target of the demonstration.

I couldn't figure out why they would picket me. I didn't want to ask for fear of having the microphone shoved into my face while I stared into the camera like a dear into headlights. Maybe that was the downfall of the animal I had taken parts of to Emilio.

I snuck out the back way and down the alley to the Plaza. I took *The Book*, as I had come to think of it. I planned to read until it was time to go to Dos Hermanas.

It was a perfect Albuquerque afternoon—an infinity of blue sky and a light dry breeze, surprisingly cool with the scent of piñon in the air.

I found a shady place and started reading. I made a valiant effort, passing my eyes over the same paragraphs hoping for some insight. None came. But five o'clock did, and I stuck *The Book* in the inside chest pocket of my jacket and went to meet Susannah.

I had decided to tell her Chris was gay. But while sitting in the plaza, I started having second thoughts. Maybe I shouldn't use the word "gay." Maybe he was bisexual. Maybe I should say he's either gay or bisexual. Then I realized that if Chris were bisexual, he still might be interested in Susannah. If so, should she know that he made a pass at me? I had no idea what to think. By the time I got there, I'd decided to say nothing.

She ordered our drinks when she saw me coming across the plaza, and they arrived just as I did. We exchanged greetings, and the salt-tinged first sip was on my tongue when Susannah said, "I wonder if Chris is gay?"

I spewed the liquid onto the table and went into a coughing spasm. Then I grabbed a napkin and started cleaning up as she asked me if I was okay.

"Just went down the wrong pipe," I lied.

"What do you think?" she asked.

"I think I'll be fine."

"I mean about Chris."

I put a chip into my mouth and shrugged.

"I've seen him four or five times and he's never so much as held my hand," she complained.

"Would it bother you if it turned out that Chris is gay?"

She thought about it while she munched a chip. "I guess not."

"You wouldn't be disappointed to pass up someone so handsome and charming?"

"Not if he's not interested in romance."

"Oh, he's interested alright,"

"How would you know?"

I took a deep breath. "Because he made a pass at me."

"No way!"

"What? You think I'm not good looking enough for Chris to make a pass at me?"

"But you're not gay."

"I guess he didn't know that."

"What did he do?"

"He kissed me," I said *sotto voce*.

"What?"

"He kissed me," I said again slightly louder.

"I can't hear you, Hubie," Susannah said impatiently. "Why are you whispering all of a sudden?"

I took a pen out of my pocket and wrote "He kissed me" on a napkin and passed it over to her.

She read it and looked up at me. "On the lips?"

"Not so loud," I pleaded, and she started laughing.

"Did you like it?"

"Shhh."

She laughed some more and it was contagious, so I started laughing too.

When we finally stopped, I told her about the protest in front of my shop.

"A protest?"

"Yeah. Several people were marching, carrying signs and chanting slogans in front of my shop."

"What were they chanting?"

"I couldn't make it out, but the signs read, 'Immigrants Deserve Justice.'"

"Huh?"

"Maybe they have me confused with that other guy."

"Which other guy?"

"You're the one who told me about him—Segundo Schuze."

She laughed and said, "I see you're not too worried about it."

There was a long silence and then Susannah said, "Thanks for telling me."

"Well, it was the first time anyone ever staged a protest directed at me."

"No, silly, not about the protest. Thanks for telling me about Chris."

"Oh." I hesitated briefly. "I should have told you sooner."

She waved it off with her free hand. "I've never been in that situation before—at least so far as I know—and neither have you, but it worked out fine. And it is sort of funny."

"I guess."

She gave me one of those smiles. "Was it a French kiss like with Lupita Fuentes?"

I angled my elbows out and rested the back of my hands on my hips. "I don't kiss and tell."

Then I violated that pledge by rehashing my Sunday evening with Dolly. Predictably, she thought it was romantic that I would date someone I went to high school with.

"But I didn't even know her in high school," I pointed out.

"That's even better. Two ships that passed in the night. Then the currents of life brought you back together many decades later."

"Not *many* decades—less than three."

She raised her eyebrows.

"Slightly less," I said.

"You know what I think, Hubie? I think you saw each other in high school and don't remember. But something stuck in your mind. That suppressed memory is what guided you back to her house on Saturday to invite her on a picnic."

"I didn't go there to invite her on a picnic. I went to ask if it was okay for Geronimo and me to have a picnic under the trees by the irrigation canal. She just misunderstood."

"Of course she misunderstood. Who goes on a picnic with a dog?"

In less than half an hour, Susannah had spun the picnic and the Sunday dinner into an epic romance, and I have to admit I enjoyed her version more than the reality. And who was to say she might not be right? I decided to call Dolly when I got home and ask her on a date.

38

My call to Dolly was delayed because the demonstration in front of my shop had grown from three or four to perhaps a dozen people, and they were louder and more enthusiastic. The signs also had new messages, saying things like "Schuze is Innocent" and "Stop Police Harassment."

The group seemed more like revelers than dissidents. They appeared to be college kids, and they were being led by a handsome young man with olive skin and dark hair hanging down in ringlets around his baby-faced head, and . . . . What the devil was Tristan doing in this demonstration?

After the television cameras stopped rolling, Tristan sent the revelers home and explained that Judge Aragon had dismissed all charges against me that morning, and that's what sparked the initial demonstration.

"I don't get it," I said. "The signs were about immigration. Why picket me? I don't have anything to do with immigration. I never even thought about it until Sunday night when I had dinner with my high school history teacher and he started talking about it."

"One of your high school teachers is still alive?" he asked playfully.

"Amazing, right? And even more amazing is the reason I had dinner with him—his daughter and I had a date."

"It's a little late to be buttering up a teacher by dating his daughter. Immigration is a hot topic these days. What did your ancient historian have to say about it?"

"He didn't say much about the current debate. He wrote a dissertation about how U.S. immigration policy between 1864 and 1893 affected the labor market of that era."

"I can't wait until the movie comes out."

"You think they were picketing me because I had dinner with Aguirre? Maybe he's involved in immigration politics."

"No, they picketed you because Segundo Cantú was an immigrant."

"But I didn't even know that."

"And the demonstrators probably didn't know you didn't know that."

"How did you know it?"

"I asked them. When I heard about the demonstration, I came down to see if you needed help. But you were gone, so I pretended to be interested in joining the protest, and they explained that Cantú was an immigrant from Mexico, and that was why the charges were dropped. They said if you had killed someone born here, you'd still be in jail."

"I didn't kill anyone born anywhere."

"I'm just telling you what they told me."

I looked at that baby-faced kid. "So you came to help me out."

He smiled and shrugged.

"Then when I wasn't here, you organized a counter demonstration."

"It was fun."

"I don't know what I'd do without you," I said.

"Aw, shucks."

"Speaking of your help, wait right here for a minute," I said and went out to the alley and came back with his garage opening wizard.

I handed it to him and said, "I don't know if you can use this thing or any of the pieces in it, but I don't want it around here."

"You sure you won't need it again?"

"Positive."

"Did it come in handy?"

"More than you know."

"More than I want to know?"

"Probably."

"Got anything to eat?"

I made a big platter of nachos. Mine are nothing like the ones you get in fast food restaurants or even most Mexican restaurants. First, I use black beans instead of pintos. Second, I use *cotilla* cheese instead of cheddar. Third, I cover the beans and cheese with caramelized jalapeños instead of the vinegary pickled ones that come in jars. I omitted the jalapeños from most of the nachos so Tristan could eat them. He went through a twelve by fifteen broiling pan of nachos in just under four minutes.

When he finally looked up from his plate, he said, "you wearing a shoulder holster, Uncle Hubert?"

I followed his gaze to my jacket and saw the bulge. "No, that's just a book I'm reading about the uncertainty principle. You know anything about that?"

"*Herr Gott würfelt nicht*," he replied.

"Huh?"

"It's a quote from Einstein. He never accepted the uncertainty principle. He believed the universe had to be predictable, so in response to the uncertainty hypothesis, he said 'God doesn't throw dice.'"

"What do you think?"

He turned up his palms and smiled. "I'm uncertain."

I called Dolly as soon as Tristan left, and I could tell from her voice she was happy I called. I wondered if she could tell from mine that I was nervous.

I know it's ridiculous, but I felt like I was sixteen again, calling Nancy Simons to ask her for a date. I'd just gotten my drivers license, and my father agreed to let me use the car so long as I was back by ten.

I asked Dolly about her dad, and we chatted about this and that for a while. When I finally worked my way around to the purpose of my call, I told her that since she had invited me for dinner, I wanted to return the favor and wondered if she might be free the next evening.

I guess my wording was a subconscious attempt not to sound like I was asking her on a date. I didn't want to feel like a high school kid. We were two mature people who had gone to the same high school. Her father had been my history teacher. She had cooked dinner for me. Now I was cooking dinner for her.

Right.

When she asked if she could bring flan, I told her I was already planning a special dessert.

"Can I bring wine?" she asked.

I must have hesitated, because she said, "You don't drink, do you? I noticed you had only coffee on Sunday."

"I'm just not fond of wine."

"Well," she joked, "If you're angling for a book, forget about it. Dad loved the one you brought, but I wouldn't have any idea what kind of book to buy for you."

"Really," I said, "you don't need to bring anything."

I spent most of the next day cleaning the house. I washed everything in the house that was made of fabric, waxed everything that was made of wood and dusted everything else.

When all that was done, I made the special dessert, a *pastel de tres leches*. I'm not a cake kind of guy, but I love *pastel de tres leches* for *tres* reasons. First, one of the three milks is heavy cream. Second, the heavy cream is mixed with rum. Third, the cake is excellent with champagne.

After the cake was done, I left the oven on and baked my famous chicken mole casserole. I admit the concept was inspired by Miss Gladys, but there are no ready-made foods in my dish. The ingredients are chicken, homemade *mole*, poblano peppers and heavy cream. The homemade *mole* involves roasting a variety of seeds, nuts, peppers, and spices and then blending them in with Mexican chocolate. I seldom make it because it's so labor intensive, but it's also a lot better than the prepared versions available in jars.

Mole is actually a healthy dish, but the casserole contains heavy cream. Between it and the *pastel*, I used an entire quart of heavy cream. I just hoped Dolly wasn't on a low cholesterol diet.

After I rested from making the *mole*, I had just enough time to shower, shave, and dress. I turned the lights down, lit the candles, and tuned my satellite radio to a station that plays a lot of Billie Holiday and Ella Fitzgerald.

If I was planning to disguise the fact that the dinner was a date, I was failing miserably.

Dolly showed up fashionably late, about a quarter after seven, in a white summery-looking and loose-fitting cotton dress with flowers embroidered around the boat neck and cuffs of the long sleeves. She smelled and looked fresh-scrubbed and had no makeup that I could discern other than faint eye shadow and lip gloss.

She was pleasantly surprised to discover that I do drink, and I was pleasantly surprised to discover that she had never heard of Gruet. Introducing her to it was fun, and she became an instant convert. She suggested we sip it in the patio.

I thought that was a good idea until I opened the door and Geronimo leapt up at Dolly, causing her to spill her champagne.

She put the empty flute down and started rubbing the dog behind his ears.

"I can't believe you still haven't found his owner," she said.

Oops.

"Well . . ." I said slowly, hoping that something would come to me so that I could finish the sentence.

"It's okay. I think I know what you're trying to tell me. You've become attached to him and don't want to give him up."

"I tried to do the right thing. I even placed an ad in the paper for a whole week."

"And you covered my neighborhood looking for his owner," she reminded me.

Except I didn't, did I? I covered her neighborhood looking for the pots. The dog was just a cover story. I felt like a dog.

"I feel guilty," I admitted.

"It's okay. Even though I wanted to adopt him, he was with you first, and you made a real effort to find his owner, so it's only fair that you should be first in line to adopt him."

She was taking it very well, and I was feeling even worse.

She suggested we have dinner in the patio, so I dragged the table outside. The candles made the patio look like an exotic resort. The chamisa that grows along the wall was fully bushed out with small yellow flowers. A light breeze pushed it against the rough adobe plaster creating a soft rhythmic brushing sound. Moonlight and candlelight played across the table, and Ella crooned from inside the house. It was about as perfect as it gets. Even Geronimo was surprisingly well behaved, almost as if he understood that I was entertaining a lady friend.

When we finally finished the meal, the dessert and two bottles of Gruet, she told me she had to get back because of her father. I put on my jacket and walked her to her car where we did what was called at Albuquerque High School in the eighties "making out." She was a lot more enthusiastic about it that Nancy Simons had been, and better at it, too.

Instead of going straight back home, I detoured to the plaza, sat down on one of the benches and stared up at the sky. It was a week or two past the summer solstice, so the Sun had started south again and the nights would be getting a little longer each day until December. But this night was spectacular with four naked-eye planets visible, three of them low in the west and the big guy, Jupiter, visible to the east.

I love the night sky in New Mexico. I watched until I got a crick in my neck, then I walked home.

39

I was in a great mood as I left the plaza, strode up to my door and started to insert the key in the lock.

I heard a vehicle approach from the east. Then I saw its reflection in the window to my left. It was a white van with black lettering on the side. It slowed. I turned. An arm extended from the window. A flare of red flame exploded from the end of the arm.

I fell to the ground unconscious.

When I came to, I was disoriented. Odd, I thought to myself, the stars are in front of me instead of above me. Someone is hovering in the sky and speaking to me. I can see her lips moving, but I can't hear anything except the ringing in my ears.

I tried to walk, but nothing happened. I tried to move my arms with the same result. I couldn't move, couldn't feel anything. I'm paralyzed, I thought to myself. I wanted to tell the person hovering over me I was paralyzed, but I couldn't speak. I wondered if I could move my eyebrows up and down in a succession of long and short movements and communicate with her by Morse code.

I couldn't move, but I could see. I knew I must be alive. There was a smell like burning flowers.

Then I was moving, headed up toward the sky. Maybe I was dying, floating away. I was turning and bouncing slightly. The sky disappeared and was replaced by a metal ceiling. Another person was looking at me and she was also speaking to me, but I couldn't hear her either.

Then I passed out again.

40

"You passed out twice?" asked Susannah. It was the next morning and she was standing by my hospital bed frowning and picking at the breakfast they brought before she came.

"I was shot! I'm lucky I only passed out instead of dying."

"You were not shot. You were shot *at*."

"I was not shot *at*. I was hit in the chest."

"No, you were hit in the book. It's a good thing the uncertainty principle is so complicated. If you'd been reading a Harlequin Romance, you'd be dead."

"I wouldn't be caught dead reading a Harlequin Romance."

Evidently she missed the humor. "What is this?" she asked, holding part of my breakfast aloft.

"Breakfast meat," I answered curtly. I thought she was taking my near assassination entirely too lightly.

"From what animal?"

"I have no idea."

She sniffed at the patty. "You were wise not to eat this. It could be dangerous."

"I'll tell you what's dangerous—being shot in the chest at close range."

"You weren't shot in the chest."

"Oh yeah?" I said, pulling up my hospital gown, "Take a look at this."

"You've got a bruise."

"A big bruise. The police told me this morning the slug they took from *The Book* was a .38 caliber."

"What does the book look like now?"

I started to complain that she was showing more solicitude for an inanimate book than she was for me, but I didn't want to be a whiner, so I took the book out of the nightstand drawer.

"Whit Fletcher brought this by this morning. He thought I might want it as a souvenir."

"Isn't this evidence?" she said as she stuck her finger into the hole that started at the cover and stopped just at the start of chapter 37.

"I guess the bullet is the evidence. They took that out already."

"It must have been one of those demonstrators who shot at you."

"But the shot came from the United Plumbing van."

"That's exactly my point. That was the van watching you during your lame 'stake-out' at Cantú's house, so it all ties together."

"What ties together?"

"Cantú was an immigrant, and the demonstrators were demonstrating against you getting off scot free after killing an immigrant."

"I didn't kill an immigrant."

She poked at the plate. "Is this round yellow thing supposed to be an egg?"

41

I was anxious to erase the event from my life, so after Susannah drove me home from the hospital, I took a long shower then ate an even longer breakfast.

I gathered all the papers from the hospital on my kitchen table and added them up, certain that the accounting department had made an error.

They had not. The ambulance service, emergency room examination, one night in a regular room for "observation," lab fees, doctors charges, and a number of petty miscellaneous charge such as a box of tissues came to just under five thousand dollars.

I wondered again about the uncertainty principle. I knew I was never going to understand it. The bullet that was headed for my heart had followed a path that was determined precisely by the angle of the gun. Fortunately, it stayed on that path and ended up in *The Book*. In chapter 37 to be exact, which was thirty-six chapters farther than I had gotten.

According to the uncertainty principle, if that bullet had been an electron, it might have swerved unpredictably, missed *The Book* and hit me directly. Of course a single electron wouldn't have left a big bruise on my chest.

It didn't make sense. The bullet, after all, is just a collection of millions of electrons and other subatomic particles. If they are all moving around at random, how come the bullet doesn't do the same?

I decided I had wasted enough time on the uncertainty principle, and I turned my thoughts to two much more practical problems—who shot me and would they try it again?

I thought about my futile search for clues in Cantú's Cadillac convertible. I remembered thinking that the difficulty was that anything could be a clue, so how would you know one if you saw one? With that in mind, I found a yellow pencil and a yellow notepad and listed everything I could think of that might be connected to my involvement with Cantú's collection and/or with my being shot.

The list ran three pages. I read over it several times. The list got shorter each time because I marked out some items that appeared on review to be irrelevant. But the list didn't just lose length. It gained coherence. I began to see how some of the things might fit together. I was developing a theory.

I heard someone knocking at the front door. When I peered through the peephole, I saw Izuanita at the door of the shop.

She still looked long and lean, and she still made me feel libidinous, but I did not open the door. For one thing, I had enjoyed my time with Dolly. For another, I didn't want Izuanita just dropping by at her convenience. I wanted her to call me. She could do that. I'm in the book.

But was she? I had no idea, but I decided to find out. If I didn't answer the door and she wanted to see me, she'd have to call.

Then what? At least I'd have her number. Or at least I would if I had one of those phones that displays the numbers of your callers and keeps a record of them. I called Tristan, and he came over with a phone that had a little screen on it.

"But if she looks me up in the book," I said, "she'll call the old phone."

He shook his head. "Your number doesn't change when you replace your land line."

"I know that. This is not the first phone I've ever had. But I thought this fancy one with the screen was like your cell phone."

"It has some of those functions, but you can ignore them. Just use it like your regular phone."

He pulled his berry phone out of a little holster on his belt and dialed. My new phone rang. His number showed up on the screen. Black magic.

42

On Sunday morning I had my normal weekend breakfast, an event that took so long to cook and so long to consume that it was noon by the time I finished.

Of course the fact that I slept until ten was a contributing factor.

After I washed the dishes, I walked to the Special Collections Branch of the Albuquerque Public Library on the corner of Central and Edith. I needed to walk off the *chorizo*, and I enjoy seeing the building, a beautiful old adobe with the traditional New Mexico palette of sand-colored stucco and turquoise doors and window trim where I spent a good deal of my youth exploring the world of information.

I would hoist a heavy volume of one of the reference works onto a massive oak table and thumb through until something caught my fancy. It was long before I learned the origin of "fancy-free," but that's what I was back then. I particularly loved reading about faraway places and the customs of different peoples. I should have guessed I'd end up an anthropologist. I think one reason travel doesn't interest me is that real travel can never measure up to the trips I took in my imagination to those faraway places.

That and the fact that I'm afraid to fly and don't like crowds.

I read a book about Einstein. Not about science, about the man. In addition to being the smartest person who ever lived (that's what the book claimed), he also had a great sense of humor. Two sayings attributed to him stuck in my mind because they seemed relevant to the theory I was developing about Cantú's pots and my being shot.

The first was, "Everything should be made as simple as possible, but not simpler." I had pared down my list of clues. What I needed to do now was put them in the simplest arrangement possible that made sense.

The second saying was, "Only two things are infinite, the universe and human stupidity, and I'm not sure about the former." Einstein's words described my situation almost perfectly. The only minor emendation I would make would be, "Only two things are infinite, the universe and *male* stupidity, and I'm not sure about the former."

When I got home, two numbers were showing on the screen. I called Tristan and he looked them up in his reverse directory. As the name implies, a reverse directory allows you to look up a number and find the person's name rather than the other way around.

One of the numbers on my new phone was from out of state, so Tristan couldn't look it up because his list is only for New Mexico exchanges. He guessed it was from a telemarketer.

The other number was a 505 area code. It was a number from Santa Fe rather than Albuquerque, and it was assigned to Oscar and Izuanita Perez.

Hmm.

While I was digesting that information, I heard a knock and looked through the peephole expecting to see Izuanita. She seemed determined to contact me. But it was Father Groaz.

"Hallow, Youbird. I heard yesterday that you had been assaulted. I went to the hospital, but they told me you had been released. You are not seriously injured?"

After I gave him the details of what happened, he smiled and said, "Too bad wass not a Bible. Would be a better story."

I told him about my conversation with Miss Gladys and the fact that she had spurned T. Morgan Fister's proposal of marriage.

"Wass probably wisdom for her to do so."

I waited for him to say something else, but he didn't, so I told him he had given me sound advice about saying nothing to her. He just nodded.

Then he came back to my situation. "Being shot is vary serious, Youbird. I know you received only a bruise, but how is your state of mind?"

"Good, I think. I know I was incredibly lucky, but I try not to read too much into that. Maybe it was the Hand of God, but I'm inclined not to see it that way. If God wanted me to keep on living, he could have done it less dramatically by just not having someone shoot at me in the first place. I don't think God needs to grandstand."

"I don't know, Youbird. Parting the Red Sea was vary dramatic."

He stared at me briefly then let out that loud belly laugh of his. When he stopped laughing, he said, "God hass a plan, but we do not know all the details. Some things happen because God makes them happen. Some things happen because He gave us free will. And some things are just luck."

I thought about that after he left. I believed someone had acted freely to shoot me, so there was the free will part. I believed the bullet hitting the book was a happy accident, so there was the luck part. I tended to believe that God had better things to do than have a bullet shot at me and land in a book, but I kept an open mind.

I called Izuanita and she said she had dropped by several times, and she asked me where I had been. She seemed a little perturbed that I wasn't at her beck and call. Then she asked how I got her phone number, and I said it showed up on my phone when she called. I told her I was sorry to have missed her and was glad she had come by. Her tone softened.

So I asked her for a date. Unlike my invitation to Dolly, I actually used the word "date."

"Sure," she said, "I'd like that."

But when I said I'd come by for her at seven the next night, she said it would be easier for her if she met me at my place. I had been hoping that Oscar Perez was her father, the two of them sharing a house and a phone number like Dolly and her father. But the fact that she didn't want me to pick her up supported the other idea I had.

She was married. No wonder she never told me where she lived. No wonder she just dropped in on me at random times without calling first. I had to hide behind my peephole pretending not to be home and use Tristan's wizardry just to get her phone number. Of course, in fairness, I'd never asked her for it. Maybe I was afraid it would seem too forward or, worse, that she would refuse to give it to me. Or maybe I had a subconscious suspicion and didn't want to know.

I have a Santa Fe phone book. I looked up Oscar and Izuanita to see where they lived. There were about two pages of Perezes, but no Oscar and no Izuanita. Their phone must have been unlisted. If it weren't for the fact that Tristan has a complete reverse directory that he got by hacking into something, I would never have found her number.

I decided that when she showed up tomorrow, I was going to ask her who Oscar is. I didn't know what answer I wanted to hear. She had accepted a date with me, so she didn't, as I had feared, see me merely as an odd but mildly entertaining shopkeeper she happened to meet. My fantasy that we might become romantically involved was actually possible. But if we did, I would have to break off my budding relationship with Dolly, and the thought of doing that made me sad. On the other hand, if Izuanita was married, I would always wonder what might have been and why she had flirted with me and agreed to a date. Was her husband an abuser? Was that why her nose was slightly crooked? Was she seeking a rescuer?

My mind continued down this path of pointless conjecture until the phone book slipped from my hand. I picked it up and opened it again.

43

Whit Fletcher walked into my shop early Monday morning and said, "You got something against the Cantú family, Hubert?"

"Well, let's see. The father stole my appraisal fee, I had to look at his corpse, and then I got falsely arrested for killing him. As far as the son goes, I didn't much like him the first time I met him, and then he disappeared when I needed some information from him. So I'm not planning to send Segundo Cantú a Christmas card this year."

"He wouldn't get it if you did. He's dead."

"I meant the son."

"He's dead too."

"That's not funny."

"Murder's never funny, Hubert."

"The son was murdered?"

"You should know," he said, and then he started reading me my rights.

I was sputtering and interrupting him but he just kept on reading.

"Come on, Whit, you already messed up when you arrested me the first time. Why make the same mistake again?"

"I didn't have nothing to do with that first arrest. In fact, I told them I didn't think you did it, but your fingerprints were on the glass with the poison in it. That's pretty good evidence. If you didn't have that slick lawyer, you'd probably be in prison now, and then you wouldn't have had the opportunity to kill the son."

The situation was so bizarre that I half believed it was a prank.

"I didn't kill the son," I said in exasperation.

"He says you did."

"How can he say anything if he's dead?"

Whit pushed a handful of silver hair off his forehead. "I got to get me a haircut. He didn't say it. He wrote it. See, after you left, he wrote a note just before he kicked the bucket. This here's just a copy."

I looked at the paper he handed me. It was a photocopy of a book on a floor. The book was open and across the print on the page were written the words, "Schuze did it."

"That book was on the floor next to him. He musta' been reading it when you shot him."

"I didn't shoot him."

"Not enough anyway. You're not cut out for this kind of work, Hubert. See, what you should have done is shoot him in the head to make sure he was dead. That first shot severed a major artery, but he probably lived a couple of minutes, just long enough to write in that book."

"I don't own a gun. I wouldn't even know how to shoot one."

"Well, you did miss his heart, but you come pretty close for a beginner."

"When was he shot?"

"Coroner's best guess is Saturday night."

"Then it couldn't have been me," I said excitedly. "I was shot Saturday night. You know that because you saw me in the hospital the next morning."

"Not this Saturday, Hubert. Last Saturday. And the thing is, not only did Cantú leave that note I just showed you, but one of the neighbors saw you coming out of the house in the middle of the night."

Oops. That was the night I had retrieved my three copies. Was Cantú dead on the floor in another room while I was retrieving my copies?

"Where did you find him?"

"In the living room, right in front of those pots, which by the way three of them was missing. But don't worry. I didn't say anything about that to anybody."

Why do these things happen to me?

I could prove Cantú was not dead on the living room floor of his father's house last Saturday because I was there burgling the place, and I'm pretty sure I would have noticed a corpse on the floor.

Although I didn't see it as burglary because the copies were mine.

"If he was killed more than a week ago and that note was next to him, how come you're just now arresting me?"

"When he was killed is just the coroner's estimate. We didn't find the body until yesterday when we got a call from a neighbor complaining about a strange smell coming from the house."

My stomach convulsed with nausea. I sat down on the stool and dropped my head into my hands. Whit brought me a glass of water. After I drank the water and my head cleared, I looked up at Whit and told him to get a chair.

He sat down next to me, and I told him the whole story, including the parts I had pieced together.

44

After Whit left, I packed a picnic basket, put Geronimo in the Bronco, and drove east through Tijeras Canyon. Then I turned north then west and took the winding road up to the crest of the Sandia Mountains.

I was about a mile from the top when the Bronco vapor locked. Those of you who began driving after the introduction of fuel injection will not know what a vapor lock is.

Come to think of it, neither do I. I just know that the carburetor stops sending gasoline to the engine, and the only thing you can do is wait until the temperature and pressure go up or down or stabilize or whatever it is they do. I left the vehicle on the side of the road. I donned a jacket and hat and walked to the summit. I was already on the massif, the steepest part of the road well behind me. But I was winded when I got to the top. It was only a mile, but oxygen is scarce at 10,000 feet.

I hiked along the rim until I came to an old bristlecone pine I'm fond of. I'm told it was growing in that spot when Caesar was ruling the Roman Empire. The oldest living thing on earth is a bristlecone pine in California dated at about five thousand years old. The one in front of me was just a youngster. Still, I enjoy seeing it, wind-swept and gnarled, impassively rooted in a harsh environment. It puts things in perspective.

I don't get up there much because it's a long and winding road and too cold and icy in the winter. There's a tramway to the crest from the west side of the mountains in Albuquerque. In fact, it's the world's longest tramway at almost three miles.

They can take it down so far as I'm concerned. There's no way I'm getting in a little box suspended hundreds of feet above the ground and held by a skinny cable. Everyone else seems to like it though.

I stared out over the Rio Grande Valley. A plaque by the tramway claims the view from up there covers eleven thousand square miles. It looks even larger. I turned back to the bristlecone for one last dose of perspective only to see Geronimo lift his leg and pee on it.

Talk about perspective.

We walked down to the Bronco to find the vapor had unlocked. I drove back to Albuquerque and my date with Izuanita.

45

"Cupid all arm'd: A certain aim he took, and loosed his love-shaft smartly from his bow, as it should pierce a hundred thousand hearts."

I remembered that phrase skipping across my mind when she'd first walked into my shop. An Aztecan goddess. A half-truth as it turned out.

She was still tall and thin with skin the color of cinnamon. Her hair was long and straight, her eyes big and dark. Her mouth was wide and her lips candy-apple red. She had long legs and long arms, and she was wearing the same sundress she'd worn that first day, revealing those same lovely long limbs.

A large cotton bag was slung over her shoulder. She took her sunglasses off, dropped them into the bag, and smiled at me.

"I don't smell anything cooking," she said teasingly.

"I was too nervous to cook."

"Then we're going out. Great. Can we take the Cadillac?"

"I'm curious," I said. "Did the Cadillac belong to your father or your brother?"

The smile slid off her face and her big round eyes narrowed.

"How did you know?"

"When you put the top down, you reached for the latches without looking for them first. You knew right where the switch was."

She smiled again. "Yeah, I had to lean over you to reach it. Did you know I was flirting with you?"

"A guy has to hope."

She laughed. "You're fun to be with, Hubie."

"You didn't tell me whose car it was."

"It was my father's." She shuddered.

"You want to tell me about it?"

"He was a bastard. I'm glad he's dead."

"Wow," I said softly.

She looked down at the floor. "He was a drug dealer in Mexico. A rival gang drove by our house one night and shot out all the windows. My mother and one of my father's bodyguards were killed. My brother and I weren't there. We were in boarding school in Santa Fe. The next week my father immigrated to Albuquerque. We've never been back to Mexico."

Only when she stopped talking did she look up.

"There was a time when I thought you killed my father."

"The police thought so, too."

"We were both wrong. I guess I knew that all along. My heart told me you couldn't do it."

"Who did?"

She looked at the hardwood again. When her face came up, tears were flowing. I handed her my handkerchief. She dabbed her cheeks then took a deep breath.

"My brother killed him. Junior was a drug addict. There's a certain poetic justice in that, don't you think? A drug dealer's son ruined by drugs. My father never had time for me, but he worshipped Segundo. When he found out he was taking drugs, he beat him. Segundo was about sixteen then. When the beatings didn't help, he put him in all sorts of programs. He'd stay clean for a few weeks, then . . ."

Her voice trailed off.

"Finally," she said, "Dad decided to simply write him off. He stopped helping him. He stopped supporting him. Segundo came to me frantic, wanted me to talk dad into giving him more money for a cure. But I knew what he wanted the money for. You could see it in those jittery eyes. Dad spent a fortune on treatments. He even bought Segundo a house in the neighborhood so he could keep an eye on him. Let him drive his precious Cadillac."

"Was it late last fall when your father cut off Segundo?"

"How did you know that?"

"Because Segundo came to my shop in December with one of your dad's pots. He paid me five thousand dollars to copy it."

"Where would he get five thousand dollars?"

"The pot he brought was worth fifty thousand. He probably agreed to sell the pot to a collector who gave him the five thousand as an advance."

I could almost see her mental wheels turning. "He needed the copy to put on the shelf so Dad wouldn't realize the original was missing."

"I wouldn't have copied it if I knew that was the plan. I thought the pot was his."

She was shaking her head as I spoke. "I had it all wrong. I thought you and Segundo were working together. He would steal the pots and you'd sell them."

"So you decided to spy on me and see what you could find out. Your husband is a plumber, right?"

She stared at me.

"It was you in that van watching me. But why? So what if your brother was ripping off your father. You said you hated him."

Her face darkened. "Those pots are *mine*, Hubert. He spent a fortune on my brother while I had to pinch pennies. Those pots were my share of the inheritance. Segundo had already gotten his half—*more* than his half. When he started in on the pots, I knew I had to stop him. I confronted him and told him I was going to tell Dad about him stealing the pots."

She spoke in a low but forceful voice, the rage contained just below the surface.

"And that's when he killed your father?"

"Yes. And ran away like the coward he's always been. He told me the whole story last Saturday. He had gone to Dad and told him you had stolen the pots and replaced them with copies. Dad bought it because apparently you have a reputation as a pot thief. He said he had a plan to trap you. He would lure you there under the guise of wanting an appraisal and they'd get your fingerprints on a glass. So when they called the police to charge you with stealing the pots, they could prove you'd been there because your prints would be on one of Dad's glasses."

"But the real plan was to frame me for your father's murder."

She nodded.

"But after he killed your father, why didn't he take the pots?"

She gave me a cynical smile I'd not seen on her before. "I'm surprised you couldn't figure that out. You seem to know everything else."

"Maybe I did figure it out. He wanted me to take the rap. If the pots are gone, they'll search my place after I'm arrested and find out I don't have them, and that will weaken their case. But if the pots are still there, their theory would be that I was going to go back later and get them. After all, it takes a lot of time to properly wrap and box twenty five valuable pots."

I was thinking I'd propounded a theory along those lines to Susannah after I found the pots weren't in the first house even though Whit had seen them *after* I was there, but my recollection was muddled by the margaritas I'd been knocking back that night.

"So your brother finally came back to get the pots, you confronted him, and he told you the whole story, even admitting he'd killed your father."

She reached into her bag.

"Why would he do that?" I asked.

"Because I had a gun on him," she answered in a flat voice.

I believed her. She had one on me. I don't know anything about guns, but I was pretty certain the gun she pulled out of her bag was a .38 caliber.

And I didn't have any books in my pockets this time to stop a bullet.

"I had to kill him, Hubie. He would have taken every penny of my inheritance. Can you imagine what it's like growing up knowing your father is a drug dealer? Knowing he was responsible for your mother's death? The only think I clung to over the years was the fact that at least I'd get something out of him when he died. And then Segundo started draining him dry. I had to kill him. I had to."

"Just like you have to kill me?"

Shoot, I thought to myself. I didn't mean it as a directive to her. I said it to myself because I was upset that when I said that dramatic line—"Just like you have to kill me"—my voice cracked. I had hoped to be calm like Bogart.

"I'm sorry, Hubie. I really do like you. But I was afraid you'd figure it out. All those years I've waited, all that deprivation I've suffered can't be for nothing."

What's he waiting for? I thought to myself. Sure, I'm wearing a Kevlar vest, but I knew from recent experience that being shot is no fun even if the bullet doesn't penetrate. I was just glad that she was aiming at my body.

Then the door to the workshop swung open, and Whit Fletcher was aiming at Izuanita's body.

"Drop the weapon, Miss."

It's a good thing I have that peephole. A second later and I would've had another bruise on my chest.

46

It was an unusually slow night at Dos Hermanas.

Tuesdays are often slow, but this was the height of the tourist season. Maybe the tourists were all riding the tramway that evening. The view is said to be spectacular at night.

"I can't believe you went along with the Kevlar vest plan," Susannah said between bites of a chip. "No offense, Hubie, but you're not much of a risk taker."

"Having her confront me with a cop looking through my peephole was a lot less risky than not knowing when and where she might try to ambush me again."

"Still, I just can't picture you standing there calmly as she pulled that pistol out of her bag."

"She told me about killing her brother. 'I had to kill him,' she said. 'Just like you have to kill me?' I replied."

I didn't tell her my voice cracked.

"I still don't understand how you figured it out."

We were on the veranda under an orange sky.

"Neither do I."

I pulled out my list of clues and waved it above the table. "I wrote down everything related to the pots and Cantú. Then I weeded it down, crossing out things that didn't seem relevant."

She scanned down the paper. "Burning tropical flowers?"

"That was the smell I remembered hanging in the air right after I was shot."

"And?"

"The burning part must have been the gun powder. It made an interesting combination with her perfume."

"Your nose really is good. Too bad your eyes are going or you might have recognized her as the driver of the van when you were on that ridiculous stakeout."

"My eyes are perfect. The only reason I couldn't make her out was I had forgotten to take off my reading glasses."

"You didn't take your reading glasses off your perfect eyes. Interesting logic."

We both started laughing. I pulled out my dollar reading glasses and put them on and stared at Angie, and we laughed even more. Then I took them off and felt around on the table for the chips, accidentally pushing the bowl. It was a sophomoric moment, but we were in that kind of mood.

When we stopped being silly, Susannah asked me about the other things on the list. She loves this stuff.

"Cassettes?" she said, looking down at the list.

"When we went to the Hurricane, she suggested we have some music. She reached into the glove compartment, pulled out a cassette, and stuck it into the player without even looking at what she was doing."

"So? The glove compartment is the first place I would have looked for a CD, and the player was right there in the middle of the dashboard."

"It wasn't a CD, Suze."

She hesitated for a moment. "A cassette. Of course. She's not old enough to be that familiar with cassettes. Wow, you noticed that?"

"Not at the time. It was only after I began to think she might be a Cantú that the cassette thing dawned on me."

She looked back at the list. "The red stuff in the back seat was her lipstick?"

"Fingernail polish, but the same shade of red."

"It says 'Her name.' What does that mean?"

"Tristan told me Cantú was an immigrant. He found that out from the demonstrators. When I later tried out the thesis of Izuanita as a Cantú, I realized someone from Mexico is more likely to give a daughter that name."

She shook her head. "That sounds like a stretch."

"By itself, yes. But remember that the theory I put together was made up of a lot of little things that individually didn't seem significant. But when they all fit together, then you have something."

She still looked dubious, and I thought of a great example.

"Think about subatomic particles," I started.

"Not that again," she pleaded.

"Each particle," I persisted, "doesn't have a definite path. But when they're all packed together to make a tennis ball, then there is a definite path. That's the way all these clues worked together."

"Lame."

Maybe it wasn't such a great an example after all.

"I just thought of something weird," she said. "Segundo the Segundo tried to frame you for the murder of his father, and his sister tried to frame you for the murder of her brother."

"And the police bought it both times. Scary."

"But Fletcher didn't go through with the arrest the second time, and I know why."

"Okay, I'll bite—why?"

"It would have been double jeopardy. You can't be charged a *segundo* time for a *Segundo's* death."

"That's pretty good. But the real reason he let me go was he bought my theory. That and his desire to make some money on those pots."

"Hubie! That's terrible. It's one thing for you to take your copies. Cantú owed you money and someone already had the originals, but taking anything else would be just plain old stealing."

"From whom?"

"From . . . from . . . hmm. I guess they technically belong to Izuanita as Cantú's only surviving child."

"Nope. The law prevents you from profiting by any criminal act. When she killed her brother, she lost the right to inherit."

"Maybe there are cousins or something."

"Not in the U.S., and I doubt that anyone from Mexico is going to show up and claim the estate. After all, he was a drug dealer fleeing a rival gang many years ago."

"So who gets the pots?"

"I have no idea. Maybe they go to the State of New Mexico lost and found. I'll ask Layton about it."

"Knowing him, he'll probably find a way to get some of them to the University and a few to Mariella's collection."

"No doubt. And maybe he'll know about some obscure law that allows the person who helps the police apprehend a dangerous felon to lay claim to the property that felon was trying to hie off with."

"Yeah, a law as obscure as the word 'hie.' Speaking of felons, what do you think will happen to Izuanita?"

"I have no idea. Maybe she'll plead insanity and get off."

She looked into my eyes trying to read me. "Is that what you want?"

I thought about it for a while. "I could say I want justice served, but maybe it already has been. The drug dealer sees his son's life ruined by drugs. The son kills the father, then the sister kills the son. Even if she gets off, her life is a mess."

"And what about you, Hubie?"

"What about me?"

"Yeah. Remember when I had that romance with the guy who turned out to be a murderer?"

"All too well. He tried to frame me for it."

"You do seem to be a popular target for frames."

"Do I need a different brand of deodorant or something?"

She laughed that off. "I worried for a while about how I could misjudge someone so completely."

"I don't think I'll worry about that for long. I know why I misjudged Izuanita—lust."

"Good to see you're taking it well."

"It helps to have another girlfriend on the horizon."

"Dolly?"

"Yeah, I have a date with her tonight."

"Maybe something more than smooching in the parking lot."

"Definitely."

"You sound pretty confident."

I couldn't help but smile. "When I invited Dolly to dinner at my house, she wanted to bring dessert, but I told her I was making *pastel de tres leches*. Then she volunteered to bring wine, but when I hesitated, she said, 'Oh, I guess you don't like wine,' and finally I told her she really didn't have to bring anything."

"And?"

"Well, I felt a little funny about saying she didn't have to bring anything—like I wasn't being gracious. So when she invited me over for tonight, I didn't want to volunteer to bring anything because she hadn't."

"You're just being your usual overanalyzing self."

"Probably. Anyway, I didn't have to ask because she said there were two things she'd like me to bring. The first was a bottle of Gruet."

I stopped and took a sip of my margarita.

Susannah knows when I'm stringing out information, but she plays along.

"And the second thing was?"

"My toothbrush."

"Wow. But won't that be awkward? I mean, what about her father?"

"He'll have to get his own toothbrush," I said, and we both signaled for Angie as we laughed.

Acknowledgments

Of the many people who assisted me in the completion of this work, I wish especially to acknowledge my wife Lai and my daughter Claire without whom none of my work would ever be completed. Also, my sister Patricia and Professor Ofelia Nikolova, two of the dedicated mystery fans who preview my books. Thanks also to Carolyn and Andy Anderson of Questa, New Mexico for their editing assistance.

I appreciate the hundreds of readers who have taken the time at signings and by email and post to make suggestions, all of which are greatly appreciated and many of which find their way into the books.

Finally, on a personal note, I have to say this book is special to me. I wrote it while spending a carefree summer in Florence, Italy thanks to my wife who was teaching there.

Or, more accurately, it wrote itself. I had the seed of an idea. Then

I sat down to write, and the view of the Ponte Vecchio, the warm Tuscan breeze and the cool prosecco worked their magic. As noted on the cover, Einstein won the Lefty Award for the best humorous mystery novel of the year. I should have made my acceptance remarks in Italian.

About the Author

J. Michael Orenduff grew up in a house so close to the Rio Grande that he could Frisbee a tortilla into Mexico from his backyard. While studying for an MA at the University of New Mexico, he worked during the summer as a volunteer teacher at one of the nearby pueblos. After receiving a PhD from Tulane University, he became a professor. He went on to serve as president of New Mexico State University.

Orenduff took early retirement from higher education to write his award-winning Pot Thief murder mysteries, which combine archaeology and philosophy with humor and mystery. Among the author's many accolades are the Lefty Award for best humorous mystery, the Epic Award for best mystery or suspense ebook, and the New Mexico Book Award for best mystery or suspense fiction. His books have been described by the *Baltimore Sun* as "funny at a very high intellectual level" and "deliciously delightful," and by the *El Paso Times* as "the perfect fusion of murder, mayhem and margaritas."

239

THE POT THIEF MYSTERIES

FROM OPEN ROAD MEDIA

Available wherever ebooks are sold

OPEN ROAD
INTEGRATED MEDIA

Open Road Integrated Media is a digital publisher and multimedia content company. Open Road creates connections between authors and their audiences by marketing its ebooks through a new proprietary online platform, which uses premium video content and social media.

CPSIA information can be obtained
at www.ICGtesting.com
Printed in the USA
LVHW022337051118
596095LV00001B/25/P